Something Borrowed

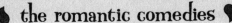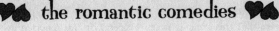

the romantic comedies

Something Borrowed

CATHERINE HAPKA

Simon Pulse
New York London Toronto Sydney

SIMON PULSE
An imprint of Simon & Schuster Children's Publishing Division
1230 Avenue of the Americas, New York, NY 10020
Copyright © 2008 by Catherine Hapka
All rights reserved, including the right of reproduction in whole or in part in any form.
SIMON PULSE and colophon are registered trademarks of Simon & Schuster, Inc.
Designed by Ann Zeak
The text of this book was set in Garamond 3.
Manufactured in the United States of America
First Simon Pulse edition April 2008
10 9 8 7 6 5 4 3 2 1
Library of Congress Control Number 2007931605
ISBN-13: 978-1-4169-5441-5
ISBN-10: 1-4169-5441-4

One

I hate pink.

Pink is the color of chewed-up bubble gum. Of scar tissue. Of Pepto-Bismol. Totally gagworthy.

Not to mention that it totally clashes with my skin tone and somehow makes my strawberry-blond hair, which I usually love, look bright orange. As a bonus, it also brings out the mud in my hazel eyes.

"It's really not that bad, Ava," my best friend, Teresa Sanchez, said. She sounded neither convinced nor convincing. In fact, I was pretty sure she'd been averting her eyes ever since I'd wriggled into the Pink Monstrosity.

I was standing in front of the mirror at Olde Main Line Bridal, staring at the baby-butt-pink, puffy-skirted satin blob my older sister, Camille, was inflicting on me for her wedding. I was Camille's maid of honor, probably due to two key facts: (1) I'm her only sister, and (2) most of her friends realized she'd drive them crazy within seconds of launching Operation Perfect Wedding. Having lived with Camille for all of my seventeen and three-quarters years, I was completely aware of both facts. I'd also figured it was pretty much a given that Camille, who was always a bit on the needy side, would morph into the Bridezilla to end all Bridezillas.

However, the pink thing had taken me by surprise. After all, Camille had known *me* for those seventeen-plus years too. You'd think in all that time she would have noticed that while pink worked just fine on her, with her blond hair and blue eyes, it was a Hindenburg-level disaster on me.

Then again, maybe I shouldn't have been surprised by Camille's complete lack of taste, considering that she had chosen Boring Bob as her husband-to-be. In fact she had dated Bob and only Bob since the dawn of time, aka middle school. Even back then, though I was just eight years old myself, I'd been thoroughly unimpressed. The thirteen-year-old Bob had been one of those kids who got out of gym a lot because of his asthma and paid a more musically hip kid to make a cool mix CD for him to give to Camille on Valentine's Day. Now, some ten years later, Bob had grown up into a total suburban metrosexual, too busy perfecting his hair-gel technique in front of the mirror to actually go out and do anything. Well, unless you counted pasta at the Olive Garden as doing something. Which I certainly didn't.

Anyway, I didn't see the appeal. But I wouldn't expect Clueless Camille to understand. Despite being sisters, the two of us had never had much in common.

I twirled in front of the mirror, trying to convince myself that Teresa was right and the dress wasn't that bad. On the plus side, it did make me look much more hourglassy than I really was, thanks to the enormous pouffy sleeves and bubble-butt skirt. Maybe my cute face and outgoing personality would be enough to pull off the look. . . .

But no. The Pink Horror was just too strong. It was even starting to overcome my natural sense of optimism and *joie de vivre*.

"Did I ever mention that I hate pink?" I mumbled with a defeated sigh.

Teresa got up and came over to stand next to me. Her reflection in the mirror looked refreshingly nonpink. Her thick dark hair was pulled back from her gorgeous-without-a-speck-of-makeup (not even concealer—talk about unfair!) high-cheekboned face. She was wearing denim cutoffs and a white fitted T-shirt with the faintest hint of faded green horse slobber on the sleeve. Even though I was standing on that little platform they always have in bridal shops, Teresa was still a bit taller than me.

"Look, Ava," she said in her best listen-up voice. She'd developed it over her years of dealing with horses, and it worked pretty well on people, too. "Unless you decide to run away from home in the next two weeks, you're going to have to show up at that wedding in this dress. So you might as well suck it up and deal."

That was just like Teresa. Despite her sultry foreign-film-star looks, she was definitely the no-nonsense, pragmatic type. I'd always appreciated that about her, especially since I tended toward the happy-go-lucky and giddily impractical myself. Or so Teresa had always told me. And she was almost always right.

That didn't mean I always had to admit it. "You're just saying that because you won't have to witness my fashion catastrophe in person," I pointed out. "I still don't know how you managed to make that happen."

She smiled serenely. "Don't be silly. I signed up for that internship way before I found out Camille's wedding date."

"Whatever. You're just going to have to deal with the fact that you're missing the social event of the season. People from Ardmore to Malvern are going to be talking about this wedding for eons, and you're going to miss it just for the chance to help a bunch of foreign horses improve their sex lives."

Teresa kept smiling. She didn't seem too broken up about the idea of missing the wedding. In less than two weeks she would be leaving for a monthlong internship on a horse-breeding farm in Germany. I'd been kind of bummed when I'd first heard about the trip. Teresa was a year older than me and had just finished her first year at the University of Pennsylvania. Even though

Penn was just a few miles up the road in Philadelphia, it had been a big change to go from seeing her every day to only on the occasional weekend. I'd imagined us making up for lost time over the summer: lots of days hanging out together by my family's pool, at her barn, at the mall; lots of evenings double-dating with our respective boyfriends.

Not that I'd been particularly looking forward to spending more time with Teresa's boyfriend. Teresa and Jason had met at a college party, and I'd disapproved practically from the moment I'd met him six months ago. I still had no idea what she saw in him. I mean, sure, he was cute. Very cute, as a matter of fact: tall, sort of tousley brown hair, great butt. Plus he was smart, with a killer smile and a quick wit. For a second when I'd first met him, I'd been almost envious.

Almost. See, it hadn't taken me long to realize that despite those surface charms, Jason was almost as Boring Bob-like as Bob himself, what with the perfect hair and the perfectly preppy clothes and that smug little smirk of his that always made me suspect he was secretly laughing at me. I wasn't sure of his feelings toward the Olive Garden, but then again I wasn't sure about his feelings about much of anything. He barely talked about himself at all and seemed to have no particular interests other than watching basketball on TV and messing around with his computer. Like I said, boring.

Despite all that, I'd been more than willing to tolerate his dullness if it meant spending more time with Teresa this summer. Of course, now we had a month less than I'd planned thanks to that internship. When I realized she would be hopping the plane for Munich exactly one day before Camille's Big Day, my wistful disappointment changed to sheer envy. Unfortunately, it was far too late by then to sign up for that internship myself—not to mention the fact that horses made me a little nervous, and they mostly seemed to feel the same way about me.

The bridal-shop woman had been busy on the phone for the past few minutes. But now she came bustling over to check on us. She was one of those quintessential Main Line ladies of a certain age: carefully frosted and coiffed hair courtesy of Toppers Spa or some such place, clothes so conservative that you just knew they had to be expensive, and a touch of plastic surgery to pull it all together.

"How are we doing over here, ladies?" she asked in what I could only describe as a brisk coo. "Miss Hamilton, the gown looks fabulous! Though I think we may need to take it in a smidge more at the bust . . ." She pulled a tape measure out of her pocket and went to work.

I fought the urge to roll my eyes at Teresa. If there's one thing even more fun than trying on a fugly pink dress, it's standing there with a complete stranger poking at your chest while basically telling you you have no boobs. Isn't that exactly how any girl would love to spend a gorgeous summer Sunday afternoon?

"Hey, Ava, I think I hear your phone ringing." Teresa glanced in the direction of the dressing room. "Want me to grab it?"

"No, thanks," I said. "Let it go to voice mail. It's probably just Mom again, complaining about Camzilla's latest breakdown."

Teresa grinned. "Right. What was it last time? Problems with the cake?"

"Keep up; that was last week. Today it

was something about canapés, I think. Mom didn't go into detail in her message, but I'm pretty sure it involved the end of life as we know it."

The bridal-shop lady glanced at us both with a sort of *tut-tut* look on her face, though she was far too well-bred to say anything. Or maybe it was because she'd met my sister and realized what we were dealing with.

It seemed like forever before the bridal lady was satisfied that, yes, the Pink Thing could be properly molded to my B-minus boobage. Finally, she stepped back and tucked away her tape measure.

"All right, Miss Hamilton," she said, "we'll be sure to have your dress ready to try on again by the next fitting."

"What if it still doesn't fit right?" I asked with a sudden burst of hope. "The wedding is two weeks from yesterday. Is there any chance it might not be ready?"

Her reassuring smile made my new-found hope fizzle out. "Our most talented seamstress will be working on it. It will fit; don't worry. Just leave it on the hook in the dressing room, and we'll see you again on Thursday for the final fitting."

"Come on, Ave. Let's go get you changed and get out of here." Teresa grabbed my hand and dragged me off the little platform. We pushed our way past a rack of plastic-shrouded bridal white and through an arched doorway into the dressing room.

In the same way that "dress" means something completely different in Bridal Shop Land, so does "dressing room." Instead of the toilet-stall-like individual enclosures you usually find at the mall, this place had just one big, open room, complete with framed wedding photos on the walls, several tasteful white upholstered sofas and chairs scattered around, and a couple of those little platforms with accompanying three-way mirrors. The day Camille tried on her gown for the first time, there had actually been another bride, her mother, and about half a dozen giggling friends in there with us. I'd expected Camille to blow her top at that, but she'd been so busy freaking out over how the (pure white) buttons didn't *exactly* match the color of the (pure white) fabric that I'm not sure she even noticed.

Today Teresa and I had the place to ourselves, and I was glad about that. The fewer witnesses to my pink shame the better. I'd dropped my clothes on one of the white tufted chairs, and they were right there waiting for me, although apparently Bridal Lady had sneaked in and folded them while we were outside. Folded or not, I'd never been so glad to see them.

Unfortunately, as I mentioned, the deluxe dressing room also included a couple of those giant three-way mirrors. That meant I was subjected once again to the view of myself encased in the Pink Horror.

"This is really going to happen, isn't it?" I asked Teresa as I stared at my cotton-candy-colored reflection. "I'm actually going to have to wear this thing in public."

"*And* be memorialized forever in the wedding photos," Teresa said. Apparently realizing it wasn't the most tactful comment in the world, she reached over and squeezed my arm. "But don't worry. If anyone can pull off the look, you can. Besides, you'll probably forget you're wearing it once the reception starts and you're dancing the night away with Lance."

"That's true." I brightened a bit at the thought. Lance and I had been together for nearly three months. As Teresa would say, that was practically a record for me, Ms. Short Attention Span. But Lance was pretty special. For one thing, he was super hot, with this spiky white-blond hair and biceps that would make Michelangelo drool. But it wasn't his looks that made me really fall for him. And it certainly wasn't the fact that he was Boring Bob's stepcousin. No, the first thing I adored about Lance was his incredible passion for cars.

Not that I was any kind of gearhead myself. I didn't even have a car of my own— my parents always said that if I wanted one, I could pay for it myself, and somehow I'd always found better things to do with the paycheck from my part-time job than spend it on boring stuff like insurance and gas. Besides, why go to all that trouble? I had enough friends with cars that I could almost always get a ride. And in a pinch my parents would usually let me borrow one of theirs as long as I promised to top off the tank.

In any case, even if my own motor didn't race at the very sight of a perfectly restored '65 T-bird, I could appreciate that kind of passion in Lance. I liked guys who had strong interests, who went out and *did* things. Okay, so after about the fourth time, those impromptu drag races weren't that exciting anymore. And maybe spending at least half our dates listening to Lance talk about rotors and spark plugs was getting a *teensy* bit dull. But even so, after almost three whole months, I was still smitten. Or at least interested enough to stick with Lance for a while—definitely through the wedding, for sure. After that, we would just have to see.

For now the important thing was that he was almost as crazy about me as he was about cars. And that he'd look awesome in a tux as long as he got the axle grease out from under his fingernails. That reminded me—I really needed to talk to him about the fingernail thing. . . .

"Turn around," Teresa ordered. "I'll get your zipper."

"Don't forget the stupid little pearl buttons at the top," I reminded her as I turned my back. "Camille had them special-ordered from, like, Zimbabwe or somewhere. If we lose any, she'll freak."

"How will we be able to tell?" Teresa joked. Her graceful fingers made short work of the pearl buttons and the zipper. "There you go. Free at last."

Well, not quite. See, the Pink Blob was

designed in such a way that it was almost impossible to shimmy it off over my hips and butt, despite the fact that I'm not exactly J.Lo in that department. That meant it had to go off the same way it had gone on: over my head.

"A little help here?" I said to Teresa. "And no comments about the SpongeBobs this time, please."

Teresa grinned but stayed quiet as she stepped forward. I just happened to be wearing a pair of garish and slightly baggy SpongeBob SquarePants panties that day. That was what happened when you let yourself get behind on laundry because you were so busy bridesitting. Still, it was one more reason I was really glad we were alone in the dressing room this time.

The Pink Horror was halfway over my head, stuck somewhere around my shoulders and completely blocking my vision, when I heard footsteps approaching from nearby. I froze, picturing Ms. Tastefully Coiffed Bridal Shop Lady walking in with a bride or two in tow and fainting dead away at the sight of my bright yellow panties.

But what I heard next was far more horrible than anything I could have imagined.

"Hey, are you guys almost done in . . ."

I yanked down the dress as fast as I could. I recognized that voice. Sure enough, Teresa's boyfriend was standing in the dressing-room doorway, slack-jawed and staring at me in all my butt-hanging-out, SpongeBob-underpanted glory.

"What are you *doing* in here, Jason?" Teresa exclaimed, horrified. "This is a women's dressing room!"

"Sorry." Jason snapped his mouth shut. We'd left him out in his Prius in the parking lot reading a book. Since neither Teresa nor I had access to a car that day, she'd sweet-talked him into playing chauffeur. "I wasn't expecting—" he stammered. Jason was the type of guy who was rarely at a loss for words. But he was now. Score one for me and SpongeBob. "That is, at the mall the dressing rooms are usually . . ."

Meanwhile, I was frantically trying to cover various body parts with pink satin. This was just my luck. I let my laundry pile up for a day or two and I end up flashing the world with the novelty panties my friends got me as a joke.

"What do you want, anyway?" Teresa asked Jason impatiently.

Jason cleared his throat. From the expression in his greenish-gray eyes, I couldn't quite tell if he was amused or frightened.

"Never mind," he said, shooting one last glance in the direction of my now-mercifully-hidden underpants before turning away. "I'll just, um, wait in the car."

TWO

My face was probably still bright red (NOT pink!) when my cell phone rang. Again.

"That's like the fifth time since we got here," I muttered, digging through my pile of clothes to find the phone. After Jason left, Teresa had helped me finally remove the Pink Eyesore, so now I was in nothing but my bra and SpongeBobs. "Even Crazy Camille can't manage to come up with that many crises in forty minutes, can she?"

"Don't be too sure," Teresa joked. "She's managed to have three breakdowns so far over the flowers alone." She started ticking things off on her fingers. "Then there was the invitation emergency, the various dress debacles . . ."

"And the canapés. Don't forget the canapés." My hand finally closed on the cool, smooth shape of my phone. It had stopped ringing by now, so I checked the return number on the last message. To my surprise, it didn't belong to either my mother or my sister. "Hey, it was Lance."

I'd tossed the Pink Horror on a chair, and Teresa got busy hanging it up and smoothing out the wrinkles. "I thought he was down the shore this weekend," she said.

"He is. He's spending the weekend in Wildwood with his buddies." I grimaced as I watched her fiddle with my dress. "That's where I'd be right now too, if it hadn't been for this stupid fitting."

I scrolled through the other messages on the phone. Except for the one from my mother that I'd already heard, they were all from Lance.

"Weird," I murmured. Lance wasn't the type of boyfriend who called me all the time just to say hi—certainly not four times in forty minutes. Especially on a gorgeous Sunday afternoon when he could be outside taking apart an engine with some of his gearhead beach buddies. Which reminded me: After a whole weekend of that, I could only imagine how gross his fingernails would look. . . .

"So? Go ahead and call him back already," Teresa said.

I nodded. Still thinking about how I was going to clean up those repulsive fingernails before the wedding, I sank down onto the nearest chair, the white brocade fabric feeling cool and scratchy on my bare legs. I punched Lance's speed-dial number, then held the phone between ear and shoulder as I grabbed my shorts and pulled them on.

The phone only rang once before Lance answered. "Yo," he said. "Lance here."

"Hey, cutie. It's me." I zipped up my shorts and reached for my T-shirt. "Sorry I didn't pick up before. I was at the bridal shop being tortured. Speaking of which, I was just thinking—how would you feel about a his and hers day at the salon the day before Camille's wedding? You know, facials and manicures, just the two of us—could be fun, right?"

"Um, I don't think so," he mumbled. "Listen, Ava. I really need to talk to—"

"All right, all right, no his and hers salon day. Check." I'd known that that one was a long shot. "But maybe—hang on a sec."

I removed the phone from my ear just long enough to shrug on my shirt. I wasn't ready to give up on my quest to make sure Lance looked as good as he could for the big day. As I'd mentioned to Teresa, this wedding was going to be a huge deal. I definitely didn't want to end up memorialized in the photos—not to mention in my family history—as the girl who showed up with Dirty Fingernails Guy.

He was talking when I put the phone back to my ear. ". . . and so I didn't think it should wait until I—"

"Hello?" I interrupted. "Sorry, I didn't catch that. Did you change your mind about the salon yet, big guy?" I used my most enticing hey-there-hot-stuff voice for the last part. Lance loved that voice—I could talk him into almost anything with it.

There was a long pause. "Um, Ava?" he said at last.

It finally dawned on me that he sounded kind of grim. "Lance? Is everything okay?" I asked with a somewhat belated rush of concern. "Wait, you didn't, like, crash your car in some stupid street race and get hurt or something, did you? Is that why you called? Are you in the hospital?"

Across the dressing room, Teresa glanced over, looking alarmed. I shrugged at her.

"No. I called to tell you I don't think this is working."

"What isn't working?" My mind was still at least partly on his fingernails. For one bizarre moment I thought he was warning me that he wouldn't be able to get them clean in time.

"You and me. I think we should, uh, maybe see other people."

The truth finally landed on me with a dizzying thud. "What?" I exclaimed, clutching the phone tighter. "Wait. Are you—are you *breaking up* with me? Seriously? I mean, *seriously*?"

Teresa finally stopped fussing with the Pink Horror and stared at me. Meanwhile, Lance was mumbling excuses and explanations, his words coming quickly, as if his usual lazy drawl had been sped up with a fast-forward button. As far as I could tell, the upshot was that he'd fallen for some fellow grease monkey who seemed to be his dream girl, and that he didn't want to string me along any longer.

"It's not you; it's me," he finished earnestly.

"Whatever." I was already over this whole conversation. Who did he think he was, anyway? What kind of guy breaks up with his girlfriend of three months *over the phone*? It made me wonder why I'd stuck with him for so long. "You've made your choice. So I guess this is good-bye."

I hung up before he could say anything else. Then I switched off my phone.

"Guess what?" I asked Teresa sarcastically.

She squeezed onto the chair beside me and put one long, slim arm around my shoulders. "Sorry, sweetie," she said. "If it's any consolation, I never thought he was good enough for you anyway."

"Thanks." I fished under the chair with my bare feet, searching for my shoes. "Can you believe him? He couldn't even wait until he got home to tell me in person."

She stood up and grabbed my shoes out from beneath a different chair. "Just as well," she said, dropping them in front of me. "You wouldn't want him to drop the bomb any closer to the wedding, right?"

"The wedding . . ." Now that the shock was starting to wear off, the truth was sinking in. "Oh my God, the wedding! I can't believe he did this to me! Not only do I have to nurse a broken heart when everyone else is all atwitter about romance and roses and crap like that—" Noticing Teresa's skeptical look, I grimaced. She knew me too well. "Okay, I have to nurse an *annoyed* heart. Is that better?"

"Much."

"Anyway, now I'm going to have to scramble to get another date for the wedding!" I didn't believe in wasting time, so I switched on my phone again. "Who should I ask? I know—Tommy!"

Without waiting for her to answer, I quickly checked the list of work phone numbers in my wallet and then dialed. Tommy was the cute new guy at work—he'd started a few weeks earlier at Wellington Gardens, the huge nursery a couple of towns over where I'd had a part-time job since I turned sixteen. Tommy was tall and broad-shouldered, with smoking Latin looks and a killer smile. He would look much better in a tux than Lance anyway, and potting soil was a lot easier to clean out from under fingernails than axle grease.

"Hold on, Ava," Teresa said, sounding a bit worried. "Are you sure you should call right now, when you just—"

"Hush, it's ringing." I cleared my throat, waiting for Tommy's husky voice to come on. Instead, it ended up going to voice mail. "Hey, Tommy," I said, after the beep. "It's me—Ava. From work, right? Remember me?" Okay, that sounded a little goofy. If he didn't remember me after working with me for almost a month, he would have to be mentally deficient. I'd helped *train* him, for Pete's sake. But there was no going back now, so I plowed on. "Listen, I have a proposition for you. Er, that is, how do you feel about big, fancy weddings? Wait, I mean . . ."

I paused and took a deep breath, a little embarrassed. Anyone who'd heard me at that moment would have thought I'd never asked a guy out before in my life. Clearly, Lance's bombshell had left me a little scattered.

"Okay, starting over," I said into the phone. "Look, I need a date for my sister's wedding the weekend after next. Dinner, dancing, free cake—could be fun. Want to go? Call me back. . . ." I left my cell number, then hung up.

Teresa was staring at me. "What the hell was that? You sounded like a blithering idiot."

That was Teresa for you. She didn't believe in dancing around the truth.

"Whatever." I jammed my feet into my shoes and stood up. "Maybe he'll think I'm charmingly ditzy. Anyway, it doesn't matter how I sounded as long as he says yes. Come on, let's get out of here."

When we left the dressing room, Bridal Lady was on the phone again, so we just waved our good-byes and headed outside. It was one of those rare perfect Pennsylvania summer days: low eighties, light breeze, negligible humidity. Still, I couldn't help feeling kind of cranky. Okay, so maybe Lance hadn't been my dream guy. It still felt pretty rotten to be dumped.

"I can't believe he did this," I grumbled, squinting into the afternoon sunshine, which was reflecting off the shiny metal bumpers of the Volvos and SUVs in the strip-mall parking lot. "Where's Jason?"

"Right over there where we left him." Teresa headed across the lot toward a shady area under a couple of trees.

Jason was slouched in the front seat of his blue Prius fiddling with his hair in the rearview. That was typical. Jason was almost as obsessed with maintaining perfect hair as the King of Hair Gel himself, Boring Bob. The windows were all down, and loud music poured out of the car's sound system.

"Do you mind, princess?" I leaned in through the passenger side window and cranked down the music. "Some of us still have functioning eardrums. Personally, I'd like to keep mine that way."

"Hey!" Jason reached over and turned it back up, though not quite as loud as before. "I was listening to that song."

I made a face. "You call that a song? What is this crap, anyway? I've never even heard it before."

Like I said, I was in a cranky mood. Actually, the music wasn't that bad. On a different day I might even have called it catchy in a cool punk-ska-retro kind of way.

"It's his new favorite local band," Teresa said, opening the car door. "They're called the Manayunk Mucus."

"Ew, what a name." I wrinkled my nose as I climbed into the backseat. "I mean, the mucus part is bad enough. But who even goes to Manayunk anymore?"

Jason glanced back at me, then over at Teresa. "Okay, I guess she's still holding a grudge," he said. "Listen, Ava. I'm sorry I walked in on you and SpongeBob just now, but it was—"

"Hold that thought," I interrupted as my phone rang. I fished it out and pressed it to my ear. "Hello?"

"Hey, Ava. It's Tommy. From the store?"

"Hi!" I smiled and shot Teresa a thumbs-up. "What's up? Did you get my message? What do you say—can you make it?"

"Not exactly." Tommy sounded apologetic. "That is—I'm already going to your sister's wedding. Do you know Millie Myers? She's Camille's sorority sister Mary Myers's cousin."

"Um . . ." I was definitely a little confused by now. "Maybe, I guess."

"Her mother and mine are old friends. So Millie asked me to the wedding. You know—as her date."

"Oh." Now I got it. But that didn't mean I had to like it. Why did Camille have to invite half the population of the Delaware Valley to her stupid wedding, anyway?

"I'm sorry, Ava," Tommy said. I could imagine his adorable face going all bummed out and his tanned forehead wrinkling with regret. "If I didn't already have a date, I'd be all over going with you. Maybe you can save me a dance?"

"Sure." I did my best to sound chipper and carefree. "Uh, thanks for calling back."

"See you at work."

"Okay. Bye." I hung up. Teresa was staring at me from the front seat. "Tommy already has a date for the wedding," I told her.

"Bummer." Teresa glanced over at Jason, who looked confused. "Ava just got dumped by that loser, Lance. She's working on finding herself a replacement date for the wedding."

I winced, wishing she hadn't told him. Jason thought he was pretty funny, and I could only imagine the obnoxiously "witty" teasing I was in for now. Probably something like "always a bridesmaid, never a date." Or a suggestion that I should just go with my good friend SpongeBob. I did my best to steel myself for what was sure to be a supremely annoying ride home.

To my surprise, though, he just shrugged. "Sorry, Ava," he said. Reaching over and punching the start button on the dashboard, he put the Prius in reverse. "I'll tell you, I'm just glad Teresa's going to be out of town so

I'm not stuck going to this thing." He backed expertly out of the parking space. "Since everyone in the world—or at least everyone on the Main Line—will be at Camille's extravaganza, I figure I'll have Burrito Moe's all to myself that night."

"You're lucky," I muttered.

I meant it too. Because even hanging out with Jason eating tacos would probably be better than being the pathetic girl in the ugly dress without a date to her own sister's wedding.

Three

I wasn't the type to wallow for very long. By the time Jason's car pulled into my driveway, I was back on track. If Lance was out and Tommy wasn't available, I would just have to find another date. After all, the Big Day was still nearly two weeks away. I figured it shouldn't take me more than two days to find the perfect date. Two hours if I was lucky.

"You could just go by yourself, you know," Teresa pointed out as I climbed out of the car.

"Go stag?" I shrugged. "I guess. But it'll be way more fun to go with someone. Especially since you won't be there. I'm definitely going to need someone around to help me make fun of my sister's Big Fat Main Line Wedding."

Jason smirked. "Nice attitude, maid of honor."

I ignored him, leaning on the passenger-side window frame to talk to Teresa. "Anyway, I'm not looking for my true love here. I just need some eye candy to walk in with. How hard can it be to find that? There are tons of cute guys around here, especially now that everyone's back home from college for the summer."

"Well, okay." Teresa didn't seem totally convinced. "Call me later and let me know what happens."

"Will do." I waved and stepped back. Jason leaned one elbow on the window and leaned out to back down the driveway. I stared at his arm, which was just muscular and tanned enough without being over-done. Nice.

Then I shuddered. After all, this was *Jason* I was ogling. My best friend's boyfriend *and* the most annoying guy I knew. Double trouble.

"Yeah, I *must* be feeling desperate," I muttered under my breath.

As the blue Prius disappeared down the

tree-lined street on its way back to Montgomery Avenue, I turned and headed inside. My family's house was a rambling old Tudor revival–style place with a big, deep porch, lots of peaked windows, and several mature shade trees in the front yard. It looked completely old-fashioned and charming from the outside, though the inside was a lot more up-to-date. The perfect combination, if you asked me.

I punched the code into the security-system number pad by the front door and let myself in. The AC was on, and it felt almost too cold inside.

"Anybody home?" I called out. There was no answer, so I kicked off my shoes and padded down the front hallway in my bare feet.

The spacious eat-in kitchen was empty but smelled faintly of scrambled eggs. There were breakfast dishes in the sink and papers scattered all over the butcher-block table. I didn't even have to walk over there to know that the papers had something to do with the wedding. Just about everything in the Hamilton house these days had something to do with the wedding.

There was a note stuck on the refrigerator with a golf-ball-shaped magnet. I walked over to read it.

At the club. Home in time for dinner. Dad

No surprises there. My father was an avid golfer at the best of times. Lately, with the increasing frenzy of talk about flower arrangements, seating charts, and whatnot, he'd all but moved into the club full-time. Not that I blamed him.

I poured myself a glass of orange juice. Then I grabbed the cordless phone off the kitchen counter, dug my little black book out of my backpack in the mud room, and headed for the sliding glass door leading out to the backyard. Dragging one of the teak pool lounge chairs into the shade of the wisteria arbor, I sat down and got to work.

It was pleasant work at first. Our backyard wasn't huge, but it was always a pretty nice place to be. It was dominated by a small but awesome free-form pool complete with rocks and a waterfall and surrounded by a flagstone patio. The arbor cast dappled shade over the grilling and dining area at one end of the pool. At the other end my parents had converted an old detached garage into a cool little pool house with a couple of changing rooms and a bathroom. A tall privacy fence covered with ivy kept the whole yard out of view of passersby and at the same time made it feel like a special, private little world. Our oasis, Mom sometimes called it.

At the moment the only things disturbing the idyllic scene were the spare folding chairs and tables that Mom always dragged out of the basement for our bigger parties. They were currently stacked neatly against the front wall of the pool house in preparation for a pool-party barbecue scheduled for one week from that very day. By then, out-of-town relatives and other guests would be starting to arrive for the wedding, and the family-and-friends gathering was meant to sort of kick off the final countdown to the big day the following Saturday.

Seeing those party chairs sitting there somehow made the whole thing more real all of a sudden. Up until now this whole wedding business had seemed kind of abstract, sort of like an enormous extra-credit school research project that was never going to come due. Time-consuming and a pain in the butt, but not really anything to worry about too much.

But now it was almost here. In just thirteen days my sister Camille—the girl I'd grown up with, the one who'd taught me to do an underwater somersault and never let me pick the TV shows when she was babysitting—was going to walk down the aisle and become a married woman. Weird.

I was so distracted by those sorts of thoughts that I didn't stress too much when the first couple of guys I called weren't available. My friend Brad from school already had a date—no surprise there, really—and my old next-door neighbor, Neil, who now lived way out in Chester County somewhere, was in England for the entire summer visiting relatives.

"Oh, well," I murmured as I hung up after talking to Neil's sister. "Strike two."

I took a sip of orange juice and waved away a pesky fly. Then I paged through my little black book. Actually, it wasn't really black. The cover was a sort of psychedelic pattern of mostly blues and purples. Inside were the phone numbers and other stats of everyone I knew. Most of my friends had gone high-tech, plugging that kind of info into their Treos or BlackBerrys, but to me there was something comforting about being able to look it all over in old-school black and white.

Aha. I spotted another likely candidate within seconds. It was Mario, a guy I'd gone out with a few times about a year earlier. We'd never really turned into anything serious, but he was a lot of fun, and I was sure he'd make a thoroughly enjoyable wedding date. I started to dial, then paused. My gaze had just fallen on the next entry in the book: Vic. He was the incredibly good-looking brother of a friend of mine from tennis lessons. I'd met him right around the same time I was hooking up with Lance, so nothing had happened between us—yet.

I bit my lip, squinting out at the glittering, breeze-tickled surface of the pool and trying to picture which of the two guys was the better bet. Mario would definitely be a blast to hang out with at the wedding, but Vic had more actual romantic potential if things went right. . . .

I needn't have worried about it. When I called, I discovered that both Mario and Vic already had dates to the wedding. So did Duncan, Jamal, Steve, and the six other guys I tried in the next half hour or so.

When Mike from my senior chem class

apologetically told me he'd already promised to go with my second cousin Stacy, I finally started to panic. This wedding was a monster! I'd been sort of joking earlier when I'd told Teresa it was going to be the social event of the season. But it was starting to look as if that might be true. Absolutely everyone I knew was going to be there, whether I'd realized it or not. And they all already had dates.

You could just go by yourself, you know. Teresa's voice floated through my memory.

Rationally, I knew she was right. I wasn't the kind of girl who wouldn't go anywhere if I wasn't hanging off some guy's arm. In fact some of the most fun I'd ever had was when I was single and fancy-free and had just showed up to a dance or a party with my girlfriends, free to dance and flirt and get to know any guy who caught my eye . . . or to just ignore guys entirely and have a blast with the girls.

But this was different. For one thing, it was true what I'd said earlier—going with someone would be lots more fun, especially without Teresa around to hang out with. Secondly, there was Lance. As I mentioned, he was Boring Bob's stepcousin, which meant he was invited to the wedding with or without me. What if he showed up with his new grease-monkey girlfriend? I wasn't too proud to admit that it would be embarrassing if he had a date and I didn't.

But I *was* almost too proud to admit the last reason, even to myself. This was a *wedding* we were talking about. It was a celebration of romance, of the human predilection for falling in love and pairing off. I wasn't sure why that made it much more imperative to be there as part of a couple, however temporary. But it did. The thought of anything else was weirdly depressing, and I hated being depressed.

Chewing my lower lip, I flipped through my book again, looking for more candidates. Before I could settle on any, I heard the sound of voices from the house. Glancing over, I saw that the canapé crusaders had returned.

Leaving the phone and other stuff on the pool chair, I headed inside. "Hi," I said. "How'd it go today?"

"There you are, Ava." My mom looked and sounded exasperated. Her neat blond bob was looking a little rough around the edges, and it was obvious she hadn't touched up her lipstick in quite a while. For Mom, that was roughly the equivalent of lying in the gutter with a half-empty bottle of bourbon and no shoes.

Camille barely acknowledged my entrance. She was in mid-rant. ". . . and if they're not going to honor their word about the salmon, I don't see why we should pay them anything!" she exclaimed. "I'm telling you, if they ruin my wedding, I'm going to make Daddy sue them until their eyes cross!"

Mom closed her eyes for a moment, then glanced at me. "I'm done," she said flatly. "Ava, you're it. I've had all the bridesitting I can take for one day. I feel like I'm part of some kind of ridiculous reality show."

"You mean *When Brides Attack?*" I suggested.

The ghost of a smile flitted across her face. "That's the one."

"Mo-*ther*!" Camille cried irritably. "I wish you would take this seriously! The wedding is only thirteen days away!"

"Trust me, I know that, Camille. I'm checking each hour off on my calendar. In blood."

I grinned, but Camille merely looked more insulted than ever at Mom's comment.

She'd never had the strongest sense of humor to start with, and the wedding had knocked what little there was right out of her.

She rounded on me. "Did you go to your fitting today?"

"No." I rolled my eyes. "I decided to skip out and hit the beach in Tahiti instead. I'm there right now having sunblock rubbed on my back by a shirtless native boy."

"Ava." Mom sounded tired. "Don't."

"Sorry. She's such an easy target." I shrugged at Camille. "I went. It's supposed to be ready in time for the final fitting on Friday. Unfortunately."

"Friday?" Camille shrieked. "The final fitting isn't *Friday*; it's *Thursday*! Oh my God, if the dresses aren't ready on top of everything else—"

"Chill!" I exclaimed. "The dress lady probably said Thursday. I don't remember. My mind was still in shock from all that pink."

"Knock, knock! Anybody home? The door was open." Boring Bob strolled into the kitchen, looking impeccable as always in his khakis and polo shirt. He was there for Sunday dinner, like the proper little future son-in-law that he was. His egg-shaped face showed the results of his latest trip to the tanning salon, and his dark hair was gelled to perfection as usual. I'd always vaguely wondered why he slicked it back like that—with his prematurely receding hairline, it made it look as if his hair were trying desperately to flee from his face. But as with most things Bob, I didn't worry about it much.

"Bob!" Mom and Camille both greeted him at the same time. Mom sounded ecstatic to see him. I think Camille was just happy to have someone new to listen to her woes.

"Yo, Bob-man," I added.

"Greetings, Hamiltons," Bob said to Mom and me. Then he walked over to Camille, brushed back her hair, and gave her a kiss on the forehead. "How's my blushing bride?"

"*Not* happy." Camille scowled at him. "The canapés are a disaster, and half the people on the guest list still haven't RSVP'd, and—"

"Come tell me all about it." Bob put an arm around her and steered her toward the sliding door.

Soon the two of them were out by the pool, visible through the big picture window in the dining area but mercifully silent thanks to the double-paned glass and the purring of the central air. Mom sank into the nearest chair, looking relieved. "What a day," she muttered.

"Just relax for a few minutes," I told her, already heading for the refrigerator. "I'll get you a glass of wine and then start dinner while you recover from your latest epic battle against the forces of Bridezilla."

"Thanks, Ava." Mom sighed and kicked off her Ferragamos. She glanced out at Bob and Camille. By now Camille was smiling and even laughing a little at whatever Bob was saying out there. "I'll tell you, I don't know what we'd do without Bob. I swear, I think he's the only thing keeping Camille from going off the deep end. The rest of us too." She glanced at my father's note, still hanging on the refrigerator, and sighed again. "This wedding is making us all a little nuts."

I had to admit that she had a point. As boring as Bob might be, he was awfully patient with my crazy sister. There was something to be said for that.

Camille may be wacked and have bad taste in most things, I thought as I uncorked my mom's favorite Pinot Grigio, *but maybe she really did pick the right guy for herself after all.*

It was a weird thought, considering my years of distaste for the Boring One. Maybe Mom was right. This wedding really was getting to all of us.

Four

"Here's our stop." I bounded for the doors as the R5 eased in alongside the platform at 30th Street Station. "Come on!"

"Slow down, Ava." Teresa swayed gracefully down the aisle of the moving train, clinging to the seat backs as she went. "They do actually slow the train down to let us off, you know. Sometimes they even stop."

I didn't bother to answer. Instead I stood in front of the doors, tapping my foot impatiently until they slid open, releasing us into a humid cloud of sulfurous stink. The few other passengers making the Monday mid-morning trip into the city dispersed across the platform. I grabbed Teresa's hand and squeezed it.

"Thanks for coming along to play wing-man," I said.

She appeared unimpressed by my gratefulness. "I don't know how I let you talk me into this. I should be at the barn today. And it's not like you need me along to pick up guys."

"Oh, come on." I grinned at her. "You can't tell me you'd rather be scooping horse poop than scoping out the hotties. Besides, I need you to show me around campus."

This was my latest plan to land myself a wedding date. If every guy in a ten-mile radius was already spoken for, that just meant I had to widen my range a little. And what better place to start than Teresa's university campus? I already knew from previous visits that Penn was virtually teeming with eligible men. Even during summer break there were bound to be a few hot prospects around.

I had the day off work and no time to lose, so I'd called Teresa first thing that morning to see if she'd go with me. I'd sort of been hoping that Jason and his Prius would come along as part of the deal, since both my family's cars were spoken for that day. Dad had a meeting in Delaware that afternoon, which meant he had driven in to his office instead of taking the train. And Mom's car was serving as the Bridemobile, as usual.

As it turned out, Jason had to work. Still, I figured maybe that was for the best. Better to be stuck taking the train into the city than be stuck with Jason the Jerk making obnoxious comments and scaring away all the cute, smart college guys I was planning to meet.

Teresa was less than fully enthusiastic about this whole plan. But she was a good friend, so there she was. She'd even advised me on my outfit. Skinny denim capris, sandals, and my favorite tie-back blue tank from Anthropologie. Cute, but not desperate.

We made the short walk over to Penn from the train station, cutting through Drexel's campus on the way. Before long we were on the corner of 34th and Walnut.

"Where should we start?" I asked, rubbing my hands together and glancing around. In one direction was a shopping center filled with college-friendly pizza and fast-food places. As I watched, a pair of buff-looking football types walked out with sodas in hand. In the other direction a slim, studious type was reading a book as he wandered slowly along toward the imposing library building nearby. Farther up the block three or four guys were in line at a mobile food van parked at the curb.

"Let's go sit on the grass in front of College Hall," Teresa suggested. "If I'm going to have to hang around watching you flirt, at least maybe I can work on my tan at the same time."

"Deal."

We headed up Locust Walk, the main pedestrian thoroughfare through the center of campus. I'd been to Penn plenty of times over the past year visiting Teresa, but today I seemed to see the place with new eyes. The antique brick and stone buildings clustered around the center lawn looked imposing yet friendly, like a bunch of wise gray-haired gentlemen sheltering the students from the urban jungle just outside. I shivered as we passed the main library, where three or four girls were hanging out on the button-shaped modern sculpture in front drinking coffee and talking—probably discussing some deep philosophical topic. Suddenly I could hardly wait to start college in the fall. Even though I wasn't going to Penn, just being there made my post–high school future feel real and scary and intriguing and awesome. If only I could fast-forward to then, skipping right past the wedding and all it entailed. . . .

I forgot about all that as we passed a couple strolling in the opposite direction. The guy had a swimmer's build and killer cheekbones.

"Whoa," I whispered, nudging Teresa in the ribs. "Check out Mr. GQ."

"Why don't you say it a little louder?" Teresa muttered. "I don't think his girlfriend quite heard you."

"Lighten up. If she did hear, I'm sure she'd take it as a compliment." I blinked as another guy came into view. Tall, dark, and handsome, with wavy hair and dimples. "Hey, how about him? He looks single. And he's totally gorgeous!"

Teresa raised an eyebrow. "Are you kidding? He looks just like Jason," she said. "You might as well just borrow the real thing."

"Yeah, right." I grabbed her by the hand. "Come on, let's go sit where we can get a good view."

We staked out seats on the wide swath of green lawn in front of the gothic-looking

College Hall. We even managed to find a spot where Teresa's olive skin could soak up the midday sun while I and my tender complexion could cower in the shade of a tree just a few feet away.

"Okay, maybe this wasn't such a bad idea after all." Teresa leaned back, tipped her face up, and closed her eyes. "Wake me up if you spot Mr. Right."

"Will Mr. Right Now do?" I asked. "Because I think I see him over there. And there. Oh, and also right over there."

Seriously, it was like being at the boy mall. Everywhere I looked, I saw attractive men near my age. Studious-looking hotties wandered past on their way to or from the library. Three or four cute hippie-throwback types were playing Hacky Sack in the grass a short distance away. Even the janitor walking by pushing a rolling garbage bin was good-looking. It was probably a good thing I wasn't doing this during the school year, because I was pretty sure my brain would have exploded.

"Okay, it looks like I'll have plenty of options here." I leaned back on my elbows. "So let's decide exactly what I'm looking for, okay?"

"Whatever." Teresa didn't bother to open her eyes.

I looked around thoughtfully. "If Lance shows up, I don't want him to think I'm trying to replace him . . ."

"Even though you are," Teresa put in.

". . . so I'm thinking no blonds." I shot her a look, which was completely wasted since her eyes were still shut. "And no, I'm not."

"Whatever," she said again.

"I might want to stay away from redheads, too, even though I think they're adorable."

That one actually made Teresa open her eyes. "Why?"

I shrugged. "Pink," I reminded her succinctly.

She rolled her eyes, then let them drift closed again. "Too bad my friend Brody went home to Colorado for the summer," she said lazily. "He would probably—"

"Whoa!" I interrupted. "Check *him* out."

Teresa obediently opened her eyes and sat up. "Which one?" she asked. "The chubby professor type? He's a little old for you, don't you think? Or are you talking about the Asian guy over by the statue?"

"Neither." I pointed. "I'm talking about *that* guy. With the hair."

"You mean Mr. X Games over there on the skateboard?" Teresa wrinkled her nose. "Um . . ."

She didn't seem impressed, which wasn't surprising. Teresa went more for the clean-cut type herself. Exhibit A: Jason. They didn't come much cleaner than that.

I watched the guy swoop closer, dodging pedestrians on his skateboard. He was impossibly tall and skinny, with a wild cloud of crazy red hair surrounding an angular, good-looking face.

"I thought you said no redheads," Teresa said.

"That was just a guideline." I didn't take my eyes off the guy as he executed a funky little pivot on the skateboard to allow an older woman to pass by. "I think I'll go say hi."

"Have fun. I'll be here."

I hopped up and hurried across the grass, jumping a little patch of flowers at the edge of the walk. Nobody ever accused me of being shy, and I wasn't about to get bashful now. The guy had stopped and kneeled down to tie his sneaker, which made it easy to catch up to him.

"Hi," I said. "I saw that move you made back there. You know, the little spin thing? Cool."

He glanced up at me, then stood up quickly without finishing with his sneaker laces. He was wearing baggy shorts and a Surf Naked T-shirt. "Thanks," he said, brushing a wad of hair out of his eyes. "You skate?"

"No. But I like guys who do." I tilted my head and smiled. "My name's Ava, by the way."

"I'm Zach. But my friends call me Zoom." He stuck out his hand, and I shook it. He had a nice handshake—steady but not too squeezy. "You go here, Ava? I don't remember seeing you around."

I shook my head. "My friend goes here." I gave a vague wave in Teresa's general direction. "I'm just visiting from the burbs."

"Cool." Zoom stepped on one end of his skateboard to flip the other end up into his hand. "So what do you girls have planned during your visit? Anything fun?"

A light breeze blew my hair into my face. I brushed it back and smiled up at him. "Maybe," I said. "We'll probably grab some lunch in a little while. Want to join us?"

"I wish I could." He kicked at a loose

brick on the walk, suddenly looking sorrowful. "I'm actually on my way to class. Summer school. Gotta make up credits from when I was in the hospital over the winter—snowboarding accident."

"Oh." I couldn't help being disappointed. Was this his way of blowing me off? Maybe I was reading him wrong, but he didn't look like the type to care that much whether he made it to class or not.

He seemed to read my mind. "I'd *totally* ditch," he said. "I mean, it's not that often I get invited to lunch by a couple of cute girls." He shrugged. "But we've got a quiz today. If I miss another one, I might not pass, and then I'm in trouble." He winked and grinned. "Especially since I already know I'm ditching Wednesday. Got a competition out in Bucks County."

I grinned back. He looked even more adorable with that playful, conspiratorial look on his face. Like a mischievous little boy in a grown-up hunk's body. "A competition? You mean skateboarding?"

"Naw." Zoom glanced down at his skateboard. "Freestyle BMX. It's one of my things." His eyes brightened. "Hey, you could come watch if you want."

"That sounds great!" I said quickly. Then I frowned. "Wait. But I can't. I have to work on Wednesday."

"Dude, blow it off!" Zoom urged me. "Get someone else to work for you. I could use a cheering section." He shot me a rakish smile. "Especially one cute enough to distract my competition."

It was tempting. He was definitely flirting with me now, and I could tell he was hooked. Hanging out with him at his BMX thing could be just what I needed to seal the deal.

Still, I knew what I had to say. "I can't. Sorry. See, I'm already taking a bunch of time off next week because my sister's getting married. But hey!" I added brightly, pretending I'd just had a brainstorm. "I don't have a date to the wedding yet. Want to go?"

"A wedding?" He looked slightly dubious. "Um . . ."

A few minutes later Zoom was skateboarding off to class—only a little late for his quiz—and I was skipping back over to Teresa. She shaded her eyes and squinted at me as I flopped down on the grass beside her.

"Well?" she said.

"His name's Zoom," I said happily. "He's really amazing. Definitely Mr. X Games, like you said."

"Who says you can't judge a book by its cover?" she murmured.

"He's even entered in some big BMX dirt-bike competition this week." I sighed, still wishing I could go watch him. "I guess he's really into that stuff. Kind of cool, don't you think? Anyway, he wants to maybe get together later in the week and hang out."

She shrugged. "Sounds good. So did you mention the wedding, or are you going to spring that on him after the first date?"

"I mentioned it. He wasn't too sure at first—the whole Main Line fancy dress-up thing isn't really his scene." I smiled proudly. "But then he said something about how life is all about trying new things, and he'd give anything a go once, as long as he could go there with me."

Teresa looked slightly confused. "So what does that mean? Do you have a date to the wedding?"

"I have a date to the wedding."

Five

"I still can't believe you came out to see me."
I licked hot sauce off my finger. "Aren't you
going to get in trouble for ditching class two
days in a row?"

"Who cares?" Zoom grinned at me
across the aqua-blue Formica table. "No
quiz today. Or tomorrow, either."

It was Tuesday, and we were having
lunch at Burrito Moe's. Zoom had called
that morning to see if I wanted to hang out.
At the time I'd been embroiled in a scintillating discussion with Mom and Camille
about ice sculptures, so it hadn't been a dif-
ficult decision. When he'd heard I didn't
have a car, Zoom had immediately volun-
teered to take the train out to see me, "since,

like, you came to my turf yesterday and all."
We'd been hanging out for a couple of
hours, spending the first part of that time
wandering around talking and window
shopping before ending up at the taco place.

Now there he was, sitting across from
me eating a plate of enchiladas, his wild hair
and groovy board shorts looking very much
at home in the casual beachfront-cantina
decor of Burrito Moe's. A girl I knew from
my childhood piano lessons was there picking up food, and she'd shot Zoom a curious
glance. *Cute,* she'd mouthed to me as she
hurried out.

She was right. Zoom was totally cute,
and so far we were really hitting it off.
Maybe everything happened for a reason.
After all, if Lance hadn't wigged out and
dumped me two weeks before Camille's
wedding, I might never have met Zoom.
Now I had a date with an Ivy League guy
with no axle grease under his nails, no family relation to Boring Bob, and every indication that he could turn into something
ongoing. Talk about turning lemons into
lemonade! The thought of walking into the
wedding with Zoom was almost making me
look forward to it for a change.

As I tried to imagine what he would look like in formal attire, my gaze wandered to his long, lanky, hairy legs, which were sprawled out halfway across the aisle. I couldn't help noticing that they sported an impressive collection of scars.

"What happened there?" I pointed to his legs. "Does one of your other hobbies involve wrestling grizzly bears or something?"

He lifted one leg and gazed down at it. "What, the scars?" he asked. "Naw, no bears involved. I got that one and that one skating." He pointed from one to the next. "This one here's from when I wiped out mountain biking a couple of years back, and the big one's from my snowboarding accident last winter. Oh, and that crooked one there was when I got attacked by a shark while I was surfing down in Jamaica last summer."

"A shark?" I wasn't sure whether to believe that one or not.

He grinned. "It was this big." He held out his hands to indicate a length of about a foot and a half. "But dude, it was *really* angry!"

I giggled, then reached for my drink to

douse the fire of my Spicy Quesadilla Special. "I thought *my* scar was bad." I held out my arm and pointed to the tiny white bump on the back of one wrist.

"Dude! Chick scars are totally hot." He grabbed my arm and pulled it toward him for a better look. When he brushed the tiny scar with the tip of his fingers, I had to fight back a shiver. "How'd you do it? Skydiving? Waterskiing?"

"Nothing that exciting. My sister pushed me into the pool when we were younger, and I hit it on the edge."

He glanced up at me with a knee-melting little half smile. "Well, I think it's sexy. A little damage makes people more interesting, right?"

"Right." We locked eyes for a long, intense moment. I was the first one to look away. "It's getting late," I said, glancing at my watch. "I should probably head to work soon."

"Bummer." Zoom shoved the last bite of food into his mouth, then slurped down the rest of his soda. "Sure you can't blow it off?"

"I'm sure. Sorry."

"How about tomorrow?" he wheedled with a winning smile. "Just call in sick or something. Then you can come watch my BMX thing. It's going to be awesome!"

I leaned over and poked him in the arm. "You're a bad influence," I teased. "It's totally tempting—really. But I'll come watch next time, okay? Especially if it's after the wedding." I stood and picked up my tray. "You know, I feel like all my plans are divided into two categories lately: BW and AW. Before Wedding and After Wedding."

Zoom chuckled. "Let me get that." He grabbed my tray from me and carried it over to the return spot along with his own. As we headed for the exit, he shot me a side-long glance. "Listen, I can't wait until AW to see you again. What time do you get off work tomorrow night?"

"Six thirty," I replied.

"Cool. I'll give you a call tomorrow and we can make a plan to do something later. What do you say?"

How could I resist? "Sounds great."

"Awesome." We were outside by now, walking through the little cement garden of outdoor seating between the restaurant and the sidewalk out front. It was hot and humid today and nobody was sitting out there. Zoom and I both sort of drifted to a stop and looked at each other.

"I guess I should go." Without taking my eyes off him, I waved a hand vaguely in the direction of the closest train station. "You can catch your ride back to the city right over there. I have to go the other way, so we should probably just say good-bye here."

"Cool. Guess this is good-bye for now, then." He leaned forward and rested one hand on my upper arm. "I'll talk to you tomorrow, Ava. . . ."

My heart was beating a little faster. I could tell he was going in for that key first kiss, and I was more than ready. His face came closer, closer . . .

"Hi, Ava! What's up?" a familiar voice interrupted loudly.

Zoom blinked in surprise and backed off. With a slight frown, I glanced over and saw Jason walking toward us dressed in Bermuda shorts and a T-shirt. As usual, he was wearing that smug little Mr. Slick grin of his.

I gritted my teeth. Talk about timing! "What are you doing here, Jason?"

"What do you think? Jonesing for some

tacos." He rubbed his stomach and glanced at Zoom. "Hey, man. What's up?"

"Not much, dude." Zoom nodded at him, then reached over and gave me a quick squeeze on the shoulder. "I'll catch you tomorrow, Ava."

"Okay." I watched helplessly as he loped off toward the train station. Then I rounded on Jason. "Nice interruption, genius."

"Sorry." He grinned, not looking sorry at all.

"Whatever." I turned and stalked off, deciding it wasn't worth the effort it would take to yell at him.

He caught up with me as I reached the sidewalk. "Hey, where are you going?"

"Work. If you'll excuse me, I'm late already." I kept walking.

"Hold on." He grabbed my arm to stop me. "Look, I was just kidding around. I'm sorry I interrupted you and Sideshow Bob back there. Why don't you let me make it up to you by driving you to work? It's a pretty long walk from here, especially in this heat."

I hesitated, then nodded. He was right about the heat—I was sweating already. "It's a deal," I said, shaking my arm free of his grip, which for some reason he'd failed to loosen even after I'd stopped. "But what about your tacos?"

"I'm not really that hungry." He fished his car keys out of the pocket of his shorts. "Come on, I'm parked over there."

Soon we were in the Prius heading for Wellington Gardens. I adjusted the AC output so it blew directly on my face. It felt kind of weird to be alone in the car with Jason. After six months I was getting used to him as a sort of accessory in Teresa's life, like her favorite cologne or her horses. Sitting next to him in the car like this was different—almost like he was a real person.

"So was that your new date for the wedding?" Jason asked.

I glanced over at him, but he wasn't looking at me. Traffic on Route 30 was snarled with shoppers darting in and out of businesses and parents picking up their toddlers at daycare, and he had his eyes on the road.

"Yeah," I said. "Zoom's a cool guy. I'm hoping he can help keep me sane while I'm dealing with my insane sister."

"Good luck with that." Jason snorted. "Teresa told me about the appetizer thing the other day."

"You mean the Great Canapé Disaster? Camille is *still* complaining about that one." I grimaced. "But it's way too nice a day to waste talking about my crazy sister. Let's change the subject." Figuring he probably wouldn't be interested in discussing how lucky I was to have met Zoom, I fished for a more mutually interesting topic. "Can you believe Teresa leaves for her trip in like a week and a half? You're probably going to miss her even more than I am, huh?"

He didn't answer. His eyes stayed focused straight ahead, even though the car was stopped at a red light. "Yeah," he said at last as the light turned green. He sped through it and pulled over to the curb in front of Wellington Gardens. "Well, here we are. Don't be too shy to tip your cab driver."

I reached for the door handle. "Here's a tip," I said. "Those Bermuda shorts make you look like my Grandpa Hamilton." I jumped out, then leaned back in before shutting the door. "Thanks for the ride, Gramps."

Half an hour later I was ringing up a flat of zinnias and idly thinking that I was glad Tommy wasn't in that day. I hadn't seen him since our little phone chat on Sunday. Even though I had Zoom now, I was still a little embarrassed thinking back on that goofy message I'd left for Tommy.

"Thanks for shopping at Wellington Gardens," I told the lady with the zinnias. "Please come again."

"Thanks," the woman said, picking up her bag and walking away.

The next customer in line stepped forward. "Find everything you need?" I asked automatically, barely glancing at him. Then I did a double take. "Oh, wow! Andy! Is that really you?"

My favorite ex-boyfriend ever was standing there grinning back at me. Andy looked even more adorable than the last time I'd seen him, almost a year earlier. He'd let his sandy-brown hair grow out a little, and he looked fitter and more mature. He was holding a pair of women's gardening gloves, but he dropped them on the counter and came around to give me a hug.

"Hi, Ava," he said into my ear in that warm, sexy voice of his. He smelled like coffee and aftershave. "How's it going?" He pulled back and gave me a once-over. "You look great."

"You, too!" I stared at him, still a little in shock at his sudden appearance.

Andy was the only guy I'd ever thought of as The One That Got Away. He was in Teresa's grade, and I'd dated him for almost five months. I'd broken up with him toward the end of his senior summer, just a few weeks before he left for Brown, telling him it was because I wasn't into the long-distance thing. But in truth that was only part of the reason. The other part was that Andy had always been a little too comfortable with illicit substances for my taste, and I wasn't sure I wanted to deal with that any longer. But I'd always sort of wondered . . .

Luckily, there was nobody behind him in line. I leaned on the counter and grinned like an idiot at him. "So what are you doing here?" I asked him.

"Running errands for my mom." He gestured at the gardening gloves.

I reached over and gave him a playful pinch on the arm. "Not that. I mean here in a more general sense. Good old PA. Teresa told me you had a job up in Providence for the summer."

"I do. But I took a couple of weeks off to visit the old stomping grounds." He smiled.

"Plus I told Mariella Farley I'd go to some big ol' wedding with her next weekend."

I should have known. "You and everybody else in the tri-state area," I said, rolling my eyes. Andy had grown up next door to Camille's high-school friend Mariella. I wasn't surprised that she'd asked him, even though he was a few years younger. I'd seen him in formalwear, and he was way beyond presentable. "But never mind that. Have you seen Sam and Davey and the rest of those guys since you've been home?"

"Not much." He cleared his throat. "I— um—don't really have too much in common with those guys anymore." At my look of surprise he smiled sheepishly. "High school was one thing, but getting wasted all the time didn't mesh too well with Ivy League schoolwork. I had a choice to make, and I decided to give that stuff up."

"Wow, that's great. I'm proud of you, Andy. Really." Just then I spotted my boss coming toward me from the seed aisle, and a pair of old ladies approaching from the other direction with an armful of flower pots. "Oops, I almost forgot I'm supposed to be working. . . ." I grabbed the gardening gloves and rang them up.

"Thanks," Andy said, his hand brushing mine as he took the bag. "I'll see you next weekend, Ava. Maybe we can catch up more then."

"For sure." I smiled at him. "Save a dance for me, okay? For old times' sake."

As he left, I blew out a long sigh. For a moment I almost wished that Zoom and I weren't getting along so great. It was tempting to imagine rekindling things with Andy now that he'd cleaned up his act, and a nice romantic setting like a wedding reception would certainly be the perfect place to do it. . . .

Too many guys, too little time. That was what Teresa always joked should be my motto in life, and maybe she was right.

"Welcome to Wellington Gardens," I said to the old ladies automatically, visions of cute guys still dancing through my head. "Find everything you need?"

Six

The next day I worked a double shift to make up for taking off for the wedding most of the following week. During my lunch break I hid out in the back of the perennials section and called Zoom.

"Dude, you just caught me," he said, sounding just as laid-back and awesome over the phone as he did in person. "I'm about to head out to the rally."

"Do you still want to get together later?" I asked.

"Totally! Been thinking about it since yesterday."

I shivered, liking the idea of him thinking about me so much. "Me too," I said. "So where are we going?"

"Do you know where Thermopylae is?"

"You mean the music club in Old City?" I absently plucked a dead leaf off a nearby scabiosa. "Yeah, I know it."

"I heard this awesome new local band is playing there tonight. Thought we could meet up there around nine. They've got totally tasty Greek food too, in case we get the munchies."

"Sounds great. I'll see you then. Oh! And good luck at your bike thing." As soon as I hung up with Zoom, I dialed Teresa to see if she—and chauffeur Jason—wanted to tag along and make it a double date. She was game, so we were all set.

I was still doing a mental happy dance over how well things were working out as I returned to work a few minutes later. Even seeing Tommy coming toward me didn't dampen my spirits. The way everything was going in my life at the moment, that awkward little phone message seemed nothing more but a distant, oddly charming minor memory.

"Hey, Ava," he said, swiping a hand through his dark hair. "Mr. Baum wanted me to tell you to go water the herbs."

"Okay, I'm on it. Thanks, Tommy." I

smiled at him and hurried off, humming under my breath and trying to figure out what I should wear for my date with Zoom that night.

Soon I was walking slowly between the wide flats of herb plants, sprinkling them carefully with the curly hose I'd pulled down from the irrigation system overhead. The plants released their fragrances in moist green waves every time I brushed them with my hand or the hose. I breathed in deeply, enjoying the mingling scents of basil, thyme, rosemary, oregano, lavender, and more.

For the first time in a while—or possibly *ever*—I was actively looking forward to my sister's wedding. Going with Lance hadn't seemed anywhere near as exciting and romantic as going with Zoom did now. I was starting to think that Lance had done me a big favor by dumping me. Our relationship had just about run its course anyway, and this way I could kick off a fun new relationship with Zoom at the wedding.

Before, all I'd been able to think about the wedding was the bad stuff: how much more hysterical Camille would be by then, how many things were likely to go wrong and send her over the edge, how idiotic I was going to look in the Pink Nightmare. But now here I was, humming cheerfully as I thought about all the fun things that day would bring. Me introducing Zoom to everyone I knew. Zoom watching me walk down the aisle with the other bridesmaids looking regal and gorgeous. (Okay, so I sort of edited the Pink Horror out of that part of the daydream.) Me and Zoom dancing at the reception, maybe sneaking out to the rose arbor behind the hall to steal a kiss or two . . .

I clicked off the hose and closed my eyes, smiling as I imagined that last tasty little scene. The wedding and reception were taking place at a luxurious old Main Line estate that had been converted into a site for such events. Its lush grounds would be in full bloom this time of year, including a famed rose garden that would serve as the backdrop for some of the formal photos. I could just imagine strolling through that darkened rose garden, hand in hand with Zoom, breathing in the heady floral scent just as I was breathing in the herbs surrounding me right now.

Okay, so Zoom wasn't exactly the Latinlover type or anything. But a wedding could bring out the romantic in anybody, right? Maybe as we wandered beneath an arbor he would reach up with one of those long, lean arms of his and pick me a perfect white rose off one of the vines. I opened my eyes just long enough to pluck a sprig of lavender to stand in for the imaginary rose. Closing my eyes again, I held it to my nose and breathed in the romantic scent. Then I tucked it into my hair and wrapped both arms around myself, swaying from side to side and humming a romantic tune. . . .

Just behind me I heard someone clear his throat. My face went hot as I realized I'd completely forgotten where I was. Could I possibly be more of a dork? I quickly yanked the lavender out of my hair, praying it was only my boss, Mr. Baum, coming by to check on me. He'd known me a long time and was likely to forgive and forget a little wacky behavior, especially considering the circumstances. Tommy, on the other hand, might take this as the final sign I was a complete loon.

"Uh, hi, Ava."

I froze in horror. That wasn't Mr. Baum's voice. It wasn't Tommy's, either.

Deciding I couldn't just stand there with my back to him forever, I forced myself to turn around. "Lance," I said, taking in his Pep Boys T-shirt and grease-stained hands. "What are you doing here?"

"Looking for you."

I rolled my eyes. Lance had a penchant for stating the obvious. Funny how that hadn't really bothered me before. In fact I'd once found it charming.

"Well, here I am." If he could do it, I could too. "So what do you want?"

He rubbed his hands together nervously, which made his biceps flex in a rather distracting way. I did my best to ignore that and stay focused on his face, which looked troubled.

"I feel bad about the other day," he said. "You know—how we left things between us. I, uh, thought maybe we should talk about it."

Wow. Lance had never been much of a conversationalist unless said conversation involved stuff like gear shifts and pistons. He *really* had to be feeling guilty about his rotten breakup technique to actually seek me out for a relationship chat. Or should that be an *ex*-relationship chat?

In any case, it wasn't my problem anymore. Why waste the time and energy?

"Sorry," I said briskly, grabbing the hose and coiling it back into its place. "I have work to do. Now if you'll excuse me . . ."

He opened his mouth as if to protest, but I didn't give him the chance. I hurried off toward the checkout area without a backward glance.

"Give me a break, Mother! How am I supposed to finalize the seating chart when we don't even have all the RSVPs yet?" Camille exclaimed. She whirled in her chair. "Daddy, will you talk some sense into her, please?"

My father had a distant little smile pasted on his ruddy face—an expression that hadn't changed since we'd all finished dinner an hour or so earlier. I suspected that while his body was still there in the kitchen in the midst of yet another bridal meltdown, his mind was somewhere out around the sixth green at the club.

I tugged at the hem of my short black skirt and sneaked a peek at my watch. At the moment the sixth green was sounding pretty good to me, too. And I don't even like golf.

"Look, Camille," Mom said. "I don't know who told you life was always going to be perfect, but it for damn sure wasn't me. Now, if you'd rather hold out for every last RSVP and risk having your guests milling around aimlessly next Saturday, I can't—"

From my spot across from Camille, I saw a flash of headlights through a side window. "My ride's here," I interrupted, jumping up and grabbing my purse. "I hate to miss all the fun, but I'll catch you guys later."

"Have a nice evening, Ava," Dad said. He sounded kind of wistful. I'm sure he would have preferred an evening out with me to staying home with the Bride of Freak-out-instein. And he doesn't even like popular music.

I was never so glad to escape from my house. I was even happy to see Jason for once.

"Whew, you guys got here just in time," I said as I climbed into the backseat of the Prius. "Hurricane Camille is winding herself up again in there."

"So what else is new?" Teresa joked. She looked totally glam in a sparkly black top, dangly silver earrings, and smoky eye shadow. She cleaned up pretty well when you could peel her out of her barn clothes.

"Okay, ladies," Jason said as he pulled out of my driveway. He cleared his throat and put on a fake-silly announcer voice. "Please keep your arms and legs inside the car. Next stop: Thermopylae!"

I stared at the back of his neck. "You seem awfully enthusiastic tonight."

"What can I say? I'm a happy-go-lucky guy." He grinned at me in the rearview. I noticed his hair looked even more perfect than usual.

"Whatever." I turned to Teresa. "Wait until you meet Zoom. He's the coolest."

I heard a snort from the driver's seat. "What?" I demanded.

"Did I say anything?" Jason said. "I'm just driving here."

"Fine," I said. "But listen—don't say anything stupid in front of Zoom, okay? He doesn't know me that well yet. So none of your oh-so-clever witticisms about my SpongeBob underwear or anything."

"Gee, I'd almost forgotten about that." Jason rubbed his chin and glanced at me again in the rearview. "I wonder if the band would let you get up onstage and flash the audience with your SpongeBobs? Or maybe you're wearing your Mickey Mouse panties today—after all, it is a special occasion. . . ."

Oops. Maybe I shouldn't have mentioned it. I decided it was time for a change of subject. "Um, so what did you two do today?" I leaned forward and grinned. "I only need the PG-rated version, please. I mean, I realize you *are* going to be apart for a whole month, so . . ."

"I told you earlier, Ava. I was at the barn all day." Teresa didn't meet my eye; she suddenly seemed very busy looking for something in her tiny black purse.

I smirked. For someone so confident and practical, the girl could get ridiculously private at the weirdest times. "Okay, then what about you?" I asked Jason. "Did you spend the afternoon working on your hair?"

He shot me a slightly peeved look. "Is that really what you think I do all day?"

"Okay, then what?"

"If you must know, I was doing some programming at my mom's office. They're having trouble with their system and she asked me to take a look."

"Really? You mean, like, computer stuff?" I was a little surprised, not to mention impressed. Jason's mother worked for one of the most successful real-estate agencies on the Main Line. If they'd called on Jason for help with their computers, he had to know what he was doing.

Finally Teresa glanced back at me. "I told you Jason is good with computers."

"I guess." Now that she mentioned it, that did ring a bell. For some reason, I'd always assumed she just meant he had a really cool MySpace page or something. "Speaking of computers, did I tell you guys that Camille fired the guy who set up her wedding website because he didn't answer the IM she sent him at six a.m.?"

For the rest of the ride into Philly we talked about the wedding and related subjects. Before I knew it we were cruising through Old City, a cool section of town over by the Delaware River. There were all kinds of art galleries there, along with interesting restaurants and fun shopping. The people you saw there were an eclectic bunch—from funky artists to ordinary local residents to clueless tourists wandering around between visits to the Liberty Bell, Independence Hall, and the Betsy Ross House.

Jason found a parking spot a couple of blocks from Thermopylae. We could hear the thumping beat of the opening act before we even got there. A good-sized crowd was milling around on the sidewalk out front, forcing passersby to dodge them by stepping into the street.

When we got closer, I squinted at the chalkboard sign out front. "Hey, it says the Manayunk Mucus are playing tonight," I said. "Isn't that the band you were listening to the other day, Jason?"

Teresa shot him a look. "No wonder you were so enthusiastic about tagging along on Ava's date tonight," she said. "I was wondering why I didn't have to talk you into it."

I was a little surprised by the coincidence about the featured band. But I was even more surprised when Zoom didn't show up by nine as he'd promised. Or by nine thirty. Or by ten.

At a quarter to eleven, I was still waiting. "What's the deal?" Teresa said into my ear. "What happened to Mr. Right?"

The Manayunk Mucus had long since taken the stage by then and were in the middle of a loud, fast-paced number. The small club was packed with fans grooving to the tunes. It was so loud and crowded that it was hard to move or think.

"Your guess is as good as mine." I shrugged at Teresa and turned away, feeling embarrassed and frustrated. Was Zoom standing me up? For real? I knew I hadn't imagined his interest in me the other day—he hadn't made any attempt to hide it. So what was the deal?

I tried to distract myself from my growing annoyance by watching the lead singer of the Mucus. The whole band was good, but the singer was electrifying. He was almost as tall and skinny as Zoom, with an A-plus butt encased in tight maroon leather and the milky-pale skin of someone who rarely sees the sun. His black hair was punked out in spikes, he wore a jeweled stud in his nose, and his voice was almost as smoky and dark as his eyes, which seemed to grab me by the throat every time they passed over me. I suspected he had that effect on everyone in the audience—or at least everyone female—but it still made my heart beat a little faster every time it happened.

Jason must have noticed me staring after a while. He leaned closer, resting one hand on the small of my back as he spoke directly into my ear. "Since your other boyfriend is a no-show, why not pick up

Mr. Rock Star instead?" he said, his breath tickling my cheek.

"Very funny," I said, dodging away from his hand. "And do you mind not feeling me up? Especially right in front of your girlfriend."

Jason raised both his hands in a surrender pose. "Sor-ry," he said. "You're awfully testy tonight, Ava. Why would that be?" He put one finger to his chin, pretending to think hard. "Oh, right. It must be getting stood up." He glanced meaningfully toward the stage, where the singer was on his knees, howling out the final note of the current song. "There's an easy solution to that, you know."

"Shut up," I muttered.

"Fine, I'm just trying to help." Jason shrugged, feigning hurt. "Who knows, bringing a guy like that might actually liven up the Prepsville wedding a little."

I knew he was joking, but I couldn't help smiling a little for the first time in more than an hour. It was sort of fun to imagine the look on Camille's face if I were to show up at her· wedding with *that* guy. I shivered as the singer's eyes locked on mine from the stage once again. He couldn't be more than a few years older than me, and Manayunk wasn't that far away. For a second I almost regretted already having a date. Why did I always spot the most interesting guys when I was already involved? First Andy, now Mr. Tall-Dark-and-Dangerous . . .

Then again, if Zoom wasn't going to show tonight, was there any guarantee he'd show up for the wedding? He did seem a little flaky. What if he stood me up next weekend, too?

"Thanks, everybody!" the lead singer yelled hoarsely into his microphone. "We're going to take a break. Be back in a few."

The band members set down their instruments, hopped down off the front of the small, battered stage, and headed toward the bar. That was going to take them right past us.

"Go ahead," Jason hissed, poking me in the back. "Now's your chance. Tell him you think he's sex-ay."

I shot an elbow back in his general direction, though he dodged it easily. I was so distracted by my irritation with Jason that it took me a moment to notice that the lead singer was almost on top of me. He stopped and looked down at me, those amazing eyes locking onto mine yet again.

"Enjoying the show, beautiful?" he asked in his husky, smoky, sexy voice.

I was a little overwhelmed by his closeness, but I did my best to keep my cool. "Yeah," I flirted back. "Keep up the good work, gorgeous."

He grinned and winked before moving on. I tilted my head and shot him my best coy smile in return.

But it was no good. My heart wasn't really in it. I was still too busy wondering what in the world had happened to Zoom.

Seven

It wasn't until late the next morning that Zoom finally answered his phone.

"Dude," he greeted me, sounding oddly breathy. "I've been meaning to call you."

"Really?" I said sarcastically. "That's funny, because I've called you about fifty times since you stood me up last night. What's the matter, are your fingers broken?"

"Only a couple. But they barely even hurt. My legs—whoa. That's another story."

"Wait. What?" I blinked, my self-righteous indignation deflating as quickly as a balloon running into an angry porcupine. "Um, I mean, what?"

"Sorry." He laughed into the phone, though it ended in sort of a cough and wheeze. "Guess the concussion's making it hard to make sense."

"Concussion? What are you talking about? Where are you?"

"Lower Bucks Hospital."

"What? Why?"

"Dude, I dunno," he replied. "That's where the ambulance brought me after I wiped out yesterday."

All too slowly the truth was dawning on me. "Wait, so you had an accident at your BMX thing and broke your fingers?" That didn't sound too bad, even with the concussion thrown in. Sure, it was less than ideal that his hand would probably be splinted in the wedding pictures. But I was sure the photographer could find a way to hide it.

"Yeah." He paused to cough and wheeze again. "Two fingers. Two legs. And, uh, like, three ribs. Maybe four—I forget what they said."

"Your legs?" I really, really, *really* hoped I'd misunderstood him. "You broke *both* your legs?"

"Listen, Ava," he said. "About that wedding. I'm not sure I can make it—the docs want me to stick around for a while. You know, for observation. Sorry. I know you were, like, psyched about it."

"That's okay. I understand." Feeling terrible that Zoom was in such bad shape, I made a mental note to send him a card and some skateboarding magazines or something. But I didn't bother trying to change his mind about the wedding. Walking in with a guy with a bandaged hand was one thing. Walking in with a black-and-blue guy on crutches? That was a whole different kind of picture, and not one I relished being part of. "Feel better soon, okay?"

". . . so Zoom is down for the count, and I'm back to the drawing board," I told Teresa. We were in Jason's car on our way to the bridal shop. It had only been a little more than an hour since my conversation with Zoom, so it was really just sinking in as I told Teresa the whole story. "I tried making a few more calls, but no luck."

"Did you call that lead singer from the club?" Jason put in. "I saw you ogling him all night. I'm surprised you even noticed your real date wasn't there."

Teresa shot him an irritated glance, then turned her attention back to me. I was slumped in the backseat picking at my fingernails.

"Listen, why are you beating yourself up about this, Ava?" she said. "Just go stag like I've been telling you."

"Yeah," Jason said. "You'll probably look better than most of the girls there. All the guys will want to dance with you."

I shot him a suspicious look. "Is that supposed to be some kind of crack about the Pink Horror?"

"Take it however you want." He smirked at me in the rearview, then returned his gaze to the road.

Even though I was pretty sure he was making fun of me, I thought about what he'd said. "You know, there will be a lot of cute, technically single guys there," I mused aloud. "Like Andy, for instance. It *would* be a lot easier to get reacquainted with him without a date slowing me down."

"There you go," Teresa said. "Freedom of choice."

We'd just turned into the bridal-shop parking lot. I recognized several of Camille's bridesmaids clustered on the sidewalk outside, chattering away at one another like a pack of overcaffeinated pigeons. At least half of them had a head start on the day, since they were already dressed in pink.

"Thanks for coming along, T." I said with a sigh. "I'm not sure I'd survive this on my own."

She smiled and unhooked her seat belt. "What are friends for? Come on, let's get this over with." She glanced over at Jason. "We should be done in about an hour."

"Okay, I'll be back—I'm going to swing by Burrito Moe's while I'm waiting. But don't worry. This time I *won't* come inside to check on you, no matter how long you take." He shot me an amused look.

Teresa and I got out of the car. As Jason drove off, Camille's friend Lissa spotted me and started waving giddily, as if I were her long-lost BFF.

"There's the maid of honor!" she cried out in her baby-doll voice. "How *are* you, Ava? And how's that adorable boyfriend of yours?"

I winced. That was fast.

"You mean Lance?" I cleared my throat. "Er, we're not together anymore."

Suddenly I was surrounded by the rest of the bridesmaids, all twittering with sympathy. "Oh, no!" Camille's sorority sister Mary exclaimed. "But you two made *such* a cute couple!"

"Don't worry, Ava," another bridesmaid assured me. I wasn't sure of her name, but I knew she'd gone to college with Camille. "Nobody will even notice you're alone on a busy day like that."

Lissa patted me on the arm. "That's right. That day will be all about Camille, anyway."

Camille and my mom arrived just then, distracting the flock of bridesmaids from my pathetic single state. Camille climbed out of Mom's car like a princess disembarking from her carriage and was instantly mobbed.

"This is *not* going to be fun," I muttered to Teresa, hanging back from the lovefest.

"Deep breaths," she advised me. "This too shall pass."

"Thanks, Queen Solomon." I sighed and rubbed my forehead.

"Come on, everybody," Camille called out, "let's go in. We have a lot to do today, and I still have to meet with the photographer later."

With a little help from Mom, she shooed us all into the bridal shop. The same woman was waiting for us. "Welcome, ladies," she said. "I have your dresses all ready—this shouldn't take long. Now, who'd like to go first?"

"Let Ava go first," Mary urged. She smiled at me with sympathy. Or was it pity? "She's had a tough week."

Camille frowned. "What are you talking about? Ava's been goofing off all week while I work my butt off."

"She means because of breaking up with her boyfriend," Lissa spoke up with that same pitying look on her face. "Poor thing—and right before the most romantic day of the summer!"

Now they were all staring at me again, as sorrowful as if my dog had just died on the same day I'd found out I had an incurable disease. I couldn't stand it anymore.

"Wait," I said. "I didn't tell you guys the rest. Yeah, Lance and I broke up. But the good news is, I already found a much better guy."

"Really?" Lissa gasped.

Camille looked suspicious. "Who is it?" she asked. "You didn't tell *me* anything about some great new guy."

"I don't tell you everything, sister dear." I tossed my head, going for a look of playful confidence. "It's a surprise. You guys will just have to wait and find out at the wedding."

Camille rolled her eyes. "Whatever," she muttered. But she was obviously too distracted to waste much energy on me. "Hey, Molly, did you remember to ask your grandmother if I could borrow her antique pearls?"

"She said yes," the bridesmaid in question answered, beaming. "Those pearls are going to look so amazing with your dress, Camille!"

Lissa giggled. "Too bad they aren't blue!" When several of us gave her confused looks, she giggled again. "You know—something old, something new, something borrowed, something blue. The pearls are borrowed *and* old. But not blue. Get it?"

I rolled my eyes at Teresa. All the wedding giddiness was making *me* blue, that was for sure.

"All right, girls." Mom glanced at her watch. "Can we keep things moving? Lissa and Mary, why don't you two go get changed first?"

As the other bridesmaids started twittering again, Teresa leaned toward me. "Is all the pink going to your head, or what?" she murmured. "Why did you tell them you have some incredible secret date for the wedding?"

I was already wondering that myself. But what was done was done.

"Because I do," I told her. "That is, I *will*—just as soon as I find the perfect guy to ask."

"How'd it go?" Jason asked as we climbed back into his car an hour and a half later. "Did you girls have lots of pink and frilly fun playing dress-up?"

"It was scintillating," Teresa answered. "The most exciting thing that happened the entire time was when that girl Molly stepped on her hem." She shot me a disapproving look. "Oh, wait. Also, there was Ava announcing to the world that she's bringing some fabulous man of mystery as her date. Too bad he's totally imaginary."

"I know, I know," I moaned. "What was I thinking? Now I have to come up with someone *really* good, or Camille's suburban gossip posse will have a fit. To that bunch, getting dumped is a fate worse than death."

"Don't let them get to you." Teresa

sounded more sympathetic this time. "They're too focused on their own lives to realize there's anyone out there who might be a little different from them. No imagination, that's their problem."

I smiled at her gratefully. No matter what she thought of my sometimes impulsive behavior, I knew she was always in my corner.

"It's probably just as well that Zoom guy is out of the picture," Jason said as he put the car into gear. "He was probably a little too edgy for that gang anyway."

"Yeah," I muttered. But I wasn't really paying attention. I was too busy scanning my mind for new ideas. "Listen, Teresa. Want to go hang out on campus again on Saturday? I had good luck there last time."

"Why bother?" Jason said before Teresa could answer. "I already found you the perfect wedding date."

"Who?" I glanced at him skeptically. "The counter guy at Burrito Moe's? I'd prefer someone older than fifteen, thanks."

"No. The lead singer of Manayunk Mucus."

I rolled my eyes. "Please. I'm trying to have a serious discussion here."

"I *am* serious." He shot me a glance in the rearview. His eyes held a bit of a challenge. "Unless he's not your type? Not safe and suburban enough?"

I frowned. "Who do you think I am—Camille? I don't go for suburban and safe."

"If you say so." He reached over and turned on the radio.

I leaned forward and poked him in the shoulder. "Hey," I said. "Who are *you* to call *me* suburban? Which of us is wearing an L.L.Bean T-shirt right now? And who just said Zoom was too edgy?"

"Just ignore him," Teresa advised me. "He's only trying to get a rise out of you."

"Yeah," Jason said, "ignore me. I'm just kidding around."

We changed the subject after that, but inside I was still stewing about what he'd said. If he really thought I was too suburban and safe to be interested in a guy like that singer, he knew even less about me than I'd thought.

As soon as I got home, I hurried upstairs and turned on my laptop. It only took a quick Google to find the official website of the Manayunk Mucus. The site had a little profile of the band members. Staring out at me from the top photo was that amazing lead singer. His name was Oliver, according to the site, and his eyes were almost as smoldering in the photo as they had been in real life. There was also a contact phone number on the site. Grabbing my cell, I dialed it. What did I have to lose?

"'Lo?" a hoarse, sleepy-sounding voice answered on the fifth ring.

"Um, hello? I'm trying to get ahold of Oliver? The lead singer of the Manayunk Mucus?"

"This is Oliver." The voice sounded slightly more awake this time.

I clutched the phone tightly. "Uh, hi," I said, taken aback. Somehow, I'd been expecting an agent or something. "My name's Ava. I was at your show last night at Thermopylae."

"Oh, really?" Now he sounded fully awake, though his voice had that same raw, smoky quality it did when he was singing. "What do you look like, darlin'? Maybe I saw you there."

"I'm about five-three, reddish blond hair," I said. "I was wearing a green flowered halter top?"

"Yeah, and a black miniskirt, right?

Sure, I remember you," Oliver said right away. "I always remember the cutest girl at every gig."

I was kind of taken aback. Sure, I was used to getting my share of notice from the opposite sex. But this was different. Or was it?

He's just a guy, I reminded myself. *One pant leg at a time, like all the rest of 'em.*

"Listen, Oliver. This might seem like a strange question . . ." Before I could lose my nerve, I blurted out my dilemma.

I hung up the phone a few minutes later feeling a little overwhelmed. For better or worse, I had a date for the following night—*and* another date to the wedding. One that was sure to make Camille's twittering pink minions faint in their pink pumps.

So there, Jason, I thought. I stared at the flickering photo of Oliver on my laptop screen and smiled.

Eight

Camille's bachelorette party the next evening was perfectly boring in a typical Camille-like way. I was glad that she and her dorky friends seemed to be having fun and all, but dirty Pictionary and karaoke just weren't my thing, and I was glad to have my date with Oliver as an excuse to duck out a little early.

I'd offered to take the train in to Center City, figuring the Main Line might be too much of a shock to Oliver's rock-and-roll system, but he'd gallantly insisted on being the one to travel. When I arrived at the local Thai place I'd picked for the date, he was at the bar waiting for me, looking smoking hot in a cool alt-rock kind of way.

"There you are." He stood up when I approached and looked me over. He pursed his lips. "Just as gorgeous as I remembered."

"You too," I said with a smile. "And boy, am I glad to see you tonight. I just came from the lamest bachelorette party in the world."

He put a hand on my back and steered me to an empty table. "What, no male strippers?"

"Hardly." I rolled my eyes as I allowed myself to be steered. "My sister is way too uptight for that sort of thing."

"Uh-oh." He arched an eyebrow and pulled out my chair. "What did I let myself in for? I signed on for a date with a hot babe, not an uptight Main Line wedding."

I grinned. "Too late to back out now," I teased. "But don't worry. I'll do my best to keep you entertained."

He laughed, showing nicotine-stained teeth and a surprisingly sweet smile. Suddenly I wondered why I'd ever been nervous about calling him. He was just a guy, like any other guy.

Well, maybe not *quite* like every other guy. Tonight he was dressed in skinny black jeans, electric-blue cowboy boots, a faded Sex Pistols T-shirt, and a tuxedo jacket with patches on the elbows. Oh, and a different nose ring—this one was an actual ring, with a tiny silver cross dangling from it.

"I know one way to liven things up at the wedding," I said, running my eyes over the outfit as he sat down across from me. "Wear *that*."

"Ah, but no," he replied. "I've got a much more interesting outfit in mind for the big day."

"Really?" I giggled. "What?"

He leaned forward, lacing his long fingers together and gazing at me. "I thought I'd start with my favorite pair of leather pants. Black, of course—after all, it's a formal occasion. . . ."

After that, the evening flew by. Oliver was really fun to hang out with. Better yet, the more I got to know him, the more I relished the thought of parading him around in front of all the stuffy Main Line gossips who would be at the wedding. I wasn't sure Oliver would ever be Mr. Right. But as Mr. Right Now, he was perfect. As the evening went on, he continued to plan and improve upon the outrageous outfit he planned to wear—it involved all sorts of leather, a few chains, some zebra-patterned silk, and even a touch of purple-glitter guyliner. Camille would definitely have him Photoshopped out of all the wedding pictures, and Boring Bob would probably faint when he got a load of him. Not to mention what Mr. Smug You're-So-Suburban Jason would say the first time he saw us together.

Suddenly I couldn't wait another whole week to see the reactions. "Hey," I blurted out as the waitress cleared away our plates and dropped dessert menus on the table. "Want to come to a pool party on Sunday?"

"A pool party?" He leaned closer and arched his eyebrow again. I'd never quite realized just how sexy an eyebrow could be. "Depends. Will it involve seeing you in a bikini?"

"Maybe, if you play your cards right. So how about it?"

"I'll be there. Just tell me where and when."

I gave him the info, silently congratulating myself for taking a chance on him. I'd never really pictured myself falling for a musician. Then again, I'd never met one quite like Oliver. Maybe this time Mr. Right Now really would end up turning into something more after all. . . .

I was in a great mood when I got home after my date. It was late—Oliver and I had hung out at the restaurant for a long time talking and laughing and drinking green tea. Then he'd driven me home in his old beater Chevy, leaning over to give me a kiss on the cheek before I hopped out. That wasn't at all what I'd been expecting from Mr. Walk on the Wild Side, and I'd found it quite charming.

To my surprise, all the downstairs lights were on in my house. When I let myself in, I saw why. Another category-five Bridezilla crisis was in full swing in the den. My father was sitting in front of the computer, grim-faced and silent. Camille, on the other hand, was decidedly *not* silent. She was wailing at the top of her lungs while pacing around in circles in her robe and fuzzy pink slippers. Her voice was reaching that pitch that only dogs can hear, so at first it was hard to make out exactly what the problem was.

I glanced at Mom for help. She was standing near the computer desk glancing back and forth from Dad to Camille with a frown on her face.

"Hey," I greeted her. "What's going on?"

Camille heard me and whirled around.

"I'll tell you what's going on!" she exclaimed. "That jerk of a webmaster really messed me up. My wedding site crashed, I can't retrieve the RSVP list *or* the gift registry, and now it won't even let me log on! Even though it's *my site*!"

"Yes," Mom said through clenched teeth. "And apparently this is such a big emergency that it can't possibly wait until morning."

I gulped. Mom had the patience of a saint. So far she'd been dealing pretty well with the yearlong process of planning this wedding, resorting only occasionally to an extra glass of wine or an especially pointed joke when things got ridiculous. But I could see that she was really getting fed up this time. This wedding was hard on all of us, but Mom was taking the brunt of it. Now it looked like it was my turn to take over bridesitting duties for a while before someone got hurt.

"No problem, people, I'm here," I said. Hurrying toward the computer, I gave Dad a poke on the shoulder. "Up you go, old man. What do you know about computers, anyway? Back in your day, didn't you still carry an abacus to school?"

Dad's grim mask cracked just enough to let out a hint of a smile. I could usually make him laugh even when he was deep in his I'd-rather-be-somewhere-else mode. "Watch it, missy," he said. "If you keep up that lip, I'll whack you with my dentures."

He stood up and stretched. Meanwhile, Camille was staring at me suspiciously. "What are *you* going to do?" she demanded. "You don't know any more about this stuff than I do, Ava."

"I'm sure she'll figure it out." Mom saw her escape, and she wasn't about to miss her chance. "Come on, Edward. It's been a long day—let's get to bed."

They fled the scene, leaving me alone with Cuckoo Camille. She was still glaring at me, as if daring me to make things even worse.

"Okey-doke," I said, planting myself in the computer chair. "Let's just see what we've got here. . . ."

But ten or fifteen minutes of fiddling didn't yield any promising results. Meanwhile, Camille was pacing again, occasionally muttering under her breath. Every time I shot a peek at her, she looked more upset. It was time for a new idea.

Luckily I had one. "I know who might be able to help us," I announced cheerfully after the umpteenth error message. "Jason! He's some kind of computer genius. Apparently."

"Jason who?" Camille asked.

There was a phone on the desk by the computer. I grabbed it and fished out my unblack book to look up the number for Jason's cell. "Jason, as in Teresa's Jason," I told Camille. "I'll call him right now—he and Teresa are probably still up making out since this is their last Friday night together before she leaves next week."

"Him?" She sounded dubious. "You mean that weird guy who's always making jokes? Are you sure he knows about Web stuff?"

"Hey, it's worth a shot, right?" I put the phone to my ear and waited. One ring, two, three . . . I shook my head and smiled, sending a silent apology to Teresa for interrupting whatever was going on.

Just when I thought it was going to go to voice mail, someone finally picked up. "Mmmflo?" a drowsy voice mumbled.

I blinked, taken by surprise. "Uh, Jason?" I said. "Hi, it's Ava. Did I—did I wake you or something?"

There was a long pause. "What time is it?" I heard some shuffling and shifting noises in the background. "Whoa—it's after midnight. What's wrong?" Jason added, suddenly sounding more awake. "Are you hurt? Is it Teresa? Did something happen?"

"No, no, everything's okay," I said hastily, trying not to notice Camille giving me the Look of Death. I could practically read the thought bubble over her head: *Everything is NOT okay! Waaaah!* Glancing at my watch, I saw that it was 12:20. "Sorry, guess I didn't realize it was quite this late."

"Oh. Well, why are you calling?"

I was pretty embarrassed about waking him up. Okay, maybe it was a little late to be calling according to strict Miss Manners–type conventions. But it was hardly the crack of o'dark thirty, either. How was I supposed to predict that a healthy college boy would be in bed so early, especially on his last weekend with his girlfriend for quite a while? Anyway, he was awake now—I figured I might as well plow ahead with my question.

"It's about Camille's wedding website. . . ." I filled him in on the problem.

"Hold on a sec," he said. "Let me log on and see what I can do."

"Thanks."

"What is it?" Camille hissed, leaning closer. "Does he know what's wrong?"

"Chill. He's checking now."

Camille isn't very good at chilling. But she did her best. She returned to pacing, only occasionally stopping to stare woefully at the computer screen or check her watch.

A few minutes later Jason came back on the phone. "Got it," he said, sounding fully awake by now and rather pleased with himself. "Try reloading it now. It should be working again."

"Cool. Let me check." I hit the refresh button. A second later the site popped up looking completely normal. Well, as normal as a floral-bordered wedding website with a big photo of Camille and Boring Bob on the home page can ever look.

"It's back!" Camille shrieked loudly enough to wake not only our parents, but half the neighborhood as well. "Oh my God, it's working again! Thank you, thank you!"

"Did you get that?" I said into the phone. "Camille says thanks."

"No problem." I could practically hear

Jason smiling through the phone. "Glad to be of service."

I hung up. "He says you're welcome," I said, vacating the chair so Camille could sit down.

She leaned over the keyboard. "This is awesome. I can't believe he fixed it so quickly. I should've just hired him to do it in the first place instead of that moron." She sounded relieved and much, much calmer than she had been just thirty seconds earlier. That was Camille for you. She can go from total hysteria to placid happiness and back again in 0.5 seconds.

"Yeah, maybe you should have," I said. "Teresa says he's great with all that computer stuff."

She paused in her keyboarding and glanced up at me. "You know, it's too bad Jason is already dating your best friend. He'd probably be a better wedding date for you than whatever secret wacko you have lined up."

"Me and Jason? You mean the same guy you called a weirdo a few minutes ago? Yeah, right."

I felt a flash of annoyance. But I wasn't sure whether it had to do with the crazy idea of me on any kind of date with Jason or if it was just guilt about the way I'd been gleefully imagining Oliver disrupting the oh-so-tasteful ambiance of the wedding.

Either way, it was too late to figure it out. I excused myself, leaving Camille bent over the computer, and went to bed.

Nine

"What's this thing? Is it coming with you?" I held up a funky-looking metal thingy with leather straps attached. It looked like a medieval torture device. Or maybe something Oliver might wear onstage.

Teresa grabbed it from me and tossed it into the other side of her tack trunk. "That's a cribbing collar," she said. "It stays here."

"Whatever." I was spending the afternoon at the barn helping Teresa pack up for her big trip. She was leaving in six days, and I knew for a fact that she hadn't even started figuring out what clothes to bring. That was typical. For Teresa horses always came first. She'd been that way since we were kids.

I wasn't particularly into horses myself. Like I said, they made me a little nervous. But at the moment they were all out in the pastures, and I had to admit it was sort of pleasant hanging out in the quiet, hay-scented barn. It was another hot, sunny day outside, but in there everything was sort of dim and sleepy. Even the dust mites floating in the sunbeams coming through the small barn windows seemed sort of lazy.

Teresa grabbed a brush and started pulling horse hair out of it with her fingers. "Hey, I almost forgot," she said. "I ran into Andy at the movie theater last night."

I perked up at that. "Andy? You mean my Andy?"

"Uh-huh." She shot me a glance. "He was there with his brother. We had a nice little chat. And guess what? Andy definitely doesn't have a girlfriend right now."

"Cool!" All along I'd been assuming that his wedding date with Mariella Farley was just a date of convenience, and I'd hoped that the fact he was willing to go with her meant he didn't have anyone serious back at school. But I hadn't been sure—until now. Good old Teresa! She had to be the best wingman ever. "I hope Mariella lets go of him long enough for me to have a dance or two at the wedding."

Teresa raised an eyebrow at me. "What about Oliver?"

"Oliver's cool." I smiled, thinking back on the previous night's date. "But I have no idea yet how serious things might get with us. So why not keep my options open for now?"

Teresa laughed. "Ava, you're hopeless!"

"What?" I pretended to be insulted. "Just because I haven't found my soulmate already like you have, you're going to kick me while I'm down?"

"Very funny." Teresa stood up and hurried down the aisle, disappearing into the tack room.

I went back to picking through the mystifying array of stuff in her trunk. As many of her riding lessons as I'd watched and as many of her shows as I'd attended, I still had no clue what most of the stuff was for.

Just then my cell phone rang. I dropped the leather strappy thingy I was holding and fished the phone out of my pocket. It was Camille.

"It's the website," she said tersely. "It

went down again. You have to call your friend Jason and ask him what I do now."

"He's not technically my friend," I said.

"Don't start with me, Ava!" she warned. As usual, she sounded a bit on edge. Or possibly over the edge. It was sometimes hard to tell. "I need you to call him!"

"I'm a little busy right now." I rolled my eyes dramatically at Teresa, who had just returned carrying a bridle or something. "How about if I give you his number and you can call him directly?"

"Fine, whatever."

For once I almost felt bad for Jason. He might be kind of annoying sometimes, but nobody deserved having Crazy Camille sicced on them. Still, better him than me, I decided as I looked up his cell phone number and recited it to her.

When I hung up, Teresa shot me a curious glance. "Why does Camille need to talk to Jason?" she asked.

"The site is down again. I figured it was easier just to hook them up directly than try to translate Bridalese into English."

"The site?"

My stomach did a weird little lurch as I realized Teresa had no idea what I was talking about. "Didn't Jason tell you about that?" I said. "Camille and I called him last night for help with her wedding website."

Teresa shrugged. "No, I haven't talked to him today."

"Oh." I felt a bit awkward. Was it weird that I'd had some midnight chat with her boyfriend and she didn't even know about it?

Before I could figure it out, I heard the clatter of hooves at the end of the aisle. I glanced over, mostly to see if I needed to move to avoid being trampled.

Then I did a double take. It wasn't because of the horse; it had four legs and a long face just like every other horse I'd ever seen. But the guy leading it in was definitely *not* just another guy—he was gorgeous!

"Who. Is. *That?*" I hissed at Teresa. "And where in the world have you been hiding him?"

She glanced over. "Oh, that's Kwan," she said. "He's new."

"Tasty," I murmured. Kwan hadn't noticed us yet, which gave me the perfect opportunity to check him out as he fussed around attaching his horse to the cross ties at that end of the aisle. "So, what's his story?"

"He's a really good rider," Teresa replied, reaching into her tack trunk for something. "He does three-day eventing, and his coach thinks he and his horse have a really good chance of moving up to prelim by the end of the season, and—"

"Teresa!" I said. "Think about who you're talking to here." I'd always been Teresa's most enthusiastic and loyal fan when it came to cheering on her riding, but I still didn't understand all the lingo. Besides, Kwan's skill in the saddle was definitely *not* what I was interested in at the moment.

She straightened up and glanced at me. "Oh. Right." She shrugged. "As far as I know, he doesn't have a girlfriend."

"Excellent. How about introducing me?"

Teresa sighed. But she knew better than to bother arguing. "Yo, Kwan!" she called, heading toward him with me right beside her. "How was your ride today?"

Kwan had been completely focused on taking off his horse's saddle. But now he glanced over at us. His face, which had been all business, was completely transformed by a dazzling smile.

"Hey, Teresa," he said. "It was good, thanks. . . ."

He continued talking, slipping into some sort of horse-related mumbo jumbo about jumps and strides and stuff. I wasn't really listening, being too overwhelmed by the fact that he was even cuter up close. He had symmetrical Asian features and spiky but still soft-looking black hair. His lean, muscular legs were encased in beige breeches and a pair of well-worn leather boots. He wasn't particularly tall, probably about Teresa's height, but he looked superfit.

After standing there politely for a while listening to the horse chat, I cleared my throat and elbowed Teresa. "Oh!" she said. "Sorry. Kwan, this is my friend Ava Hamilton. Ava, this is Kwan."

"Nice to meet you, Ava. Hamilton?" Kwan said quizzically as he ducked under the cross tie and stuck out his hand. "Why does that name sound so familiar?"

I shook his hand. "I don't know. I'm sure we've never met before—I would definitely remember."

My flirtatious comment appeared to fly right over his head. He had a thoughtful look on his face, obviously trying to puzzle out the connection. Nice. I liked smart, thoughtful guys.

"So you do the horse-jumping thing, huh, Kwan?" I commented.

Teresa rolled her eyes. "Ava isn't really a horse person," she told him.

"I've got it!" he exclaimed, seemingly unaware of what we'd just said. "Hamilton— are you related to Camille Hamilton?"

"Yeah, she's my older sister," I said. "Do you know her?"

He smiled, seeming quite pleased with himself for solving the mystery. "I've never met her," he said, stepping back to give his horse a pat on the neck. "But I'm going to her wedding next weekend."

What a surprise. Only not. "Oh," I said. "Are you a friend of the groom?" If he turned out to be one of Boring Bob's best boring buddies, even being superhot might not be enough to redeem him.

"No, I've never met him, either." Kwan shrugged. "A girl here at the barn is going and asked me to come as her date. Ashley Weiss," he added, with a glance at Teresa. Then he returned his smile to me. "Small world, huh?"

"The smallest." I knew Ashley Weiss, sort of. Her dad and mine played golf together, she'd taken piano lessons with

Camille for a while, and she spent every summer working part-time at Teresa's barn.

"Well, we'd better let you finish getting him untacked and cooled out." Teresa nodded toward the horse. "Come on, Ava."

"Great to meet you, Kwan," I called as she dragged me off down the aisle.

"Same here. I'll see you around, Ava."

"Definitely."

Back at her trunk, Teresa grabbed some smelly saddle pads and shoved them into my arms. "Come on," she said. "Let's go wash these."

She grabbed a few more pads and some cloth bandages, then led the way to the stable office, which was deserted. There was a washing machine in the back room, and we soon had her stuff loaded in.

"So what did you think of Kwan?" Teresa asked as she dumped in some detergent. "I probably should have thought of him the other day when you were desperate for a wedding date. I didn't know he was already going."

"Do you think it's a real date?" I asked. "Him and Ashley, I mean."

She turned on the washer and turned to me with a smile. "I doubt it, Ms. Short

Attention Span," she said. "Maybe you need to add Kwan to your dance schedule along with Oliver and Andy."

I stuck out my tongue at her. "Maybe I will," I said. "You know, I'm starting to think Lance did me a big favor by dumping me. Because Pink Horror and Crackpot Camille aside, this wedding is starting to look like a lot more fun than I ever would have expected!"

Ten

"Everything's going great, Mom," I said. "Why don't you go get yourself a drink and relax?"

"Thanks, Ava. Maybe I should do that." Still, she kept compulsively smoothing out the miniscule wrinkles in the linen tablecloth spread on one of the folding tables under the wisteria arbor.

I sighed, knowing it was hopeless. Mom was a great hostess—everyone said so—but she never really enjoyed her own parties until they were over. At least it was easy to tell where Camille had come by her OCD tendencies.

"Okay. I'm going to hang out with Teresa," I said. "Call me if you need me."

The backyard pool-party barbecue was in full swing. The place looked great—very tasteful, if perhaps slightly boring. In other words, perfect for Camille. Sprays of pink and white lilies decorated the white-dressed tables. Various friends and relatives were chatting and laughing and nibbling at an impressive range of hors d'ouevres. Camille was perched on a stool near the lilac bush talking with some friends. Bob was over near the bar nodding and smiling at one of my uncle Phil's meandering stories and pretending not to notice that Phil's gin and tonic was sloshing out of his glass as he waved his hands around. Dad was holding court over at his fancy new Weber grill, looking more cheerful than I'd seen him in a while. The scents of chlorine, sizzling shrimp, and alcohol mingled in a surprisingly pleasant way on the soft summer breeze. The weather was perfect, and several of my youngest relatives were already shouting and splashing one another in the pool.

Teresa and Jason were perched on a chaise lounge in the shade of a large potted palm. I wandered over.

"Is Oliver here yet?" Teresa asked, squinting and shading her eyes as she looked up at me. She looked downright gorgeous in a red bathing suit, black shorts, and a gauzy white button-down overshirt.

"Not yet." I grabbed Jason's arm and checked his watch. He had dressed for the occasion too, in preppy navy-blue swim trunks and a crisp white polo. "He should be here any minute now."

"Uh-oh." Jason pretended to look concerned as he yanked his arm back. "I hope you don't get stood up." He smirked. "Again."

Deciding not to dignify that with a response, I busied myself adjusting the front tie on my silver-studded black bikini top. I had dressed carefully that morning, trying to strike a balance between dutiful Main Line daughter and rebellious rock chick. I'd settled for olive cargo shorts, metallic silver flip flops and the black bikini, which I'd scored at a clearance sale at a funky little shop in Philly the previous summer but never worn until now.

When I looked up, I caught Jason staring. I blushed, realizing I was getting a little careless around him. He might be Teresa's boyfriend, but he was still a guy. Seeing me in those SpongeBob underpants had been bad enough, and here I was practically flashing him right in front of his face. . . .

I was distracted from such thoughts by a commotion from near the gate leading in from the driveway. Glancing over there, I smiled.

"Look," I said. "There's Oliver."

I hurried toward him. He was dressed in baggy black swim trunks that came down to his knees and a crazy retro Hawaiian shirt unbuttoned far enough to reveal a tangle of chains around his neck. His hair looked even cooler than usual thanks to a new electric-blue streak on one side. A camouflage-print messenger bag was slung across his chest. And today his nose piercing sported a tiny skull and crossbones. Needless to say, half the party had already turned to stare at him.

"Oh my God," I heard Camille mutter as I rushed past her. "Don't tell me . . ."

I smiled to myself. Mission accomplished!

"There you are!" I exclaimed as I reached Oliver. "I'm so glad you came."

"Me too," he purred, taking both my hands and letting his gaze wander all over me. "You look absolutely luscious!"

"Thanks." I smiled as he leaned down

and planted a kiss on my forehead. "Come on in and meet everybody."

Most of the partygoers were too polite to stare for very long. But I could tell that they were wondering who had let this alien creature into their tasteful little party. I started introducing him to various people as we walked in, including my mother, who was hurrying past with a plate of mini crab cakes.

"This is Oliver, Mom," I said. "He's the musician I told you about."

"Nice to meet you, Mrs. H." Since her hands were full, Oliver gave a little bow. "Awesome party."

Most people never would have noticed her gaze flick briefly from his nose ring to his blue hair streak before settling back on his face. Her polite smile never wavered.

"Lovely to meet you, Oliver," she said in her best gracious-hostess voice. "Any friend of Ava's is welcome here."

"Thanks, Mom. Come on," I said, taking Oliver's hand. "I want you to meet my friend Teresa."

I looked around for her. She and Jason had moved over to the edge of the pool, where they were talking with a tall, broad-shouldered African-American guy with killer abs and a buzz cut. I recognized him immediately—there's just no mistaking a physique like that.

"Hey, Rocco!" I greeted him as Oliver and I joined the little group. "I'm so glad you came!"

"Are you kidding?" Rocco said as he reached down to give me a hug. "You know I never turn down free food."

I'd been casual friends with Rocco forever; somehow we'd just never gotten around to dating each other. Everyone at school called him Rocco the Jocko. He was great at just about every sport there was and had even made the varsity football team as a freshman.

Rocco looked even hotter than usual in his sporty maroon trunks, but I hardly noticed. Most of my attention was taken up with Oliver—I was totally aware of him standing there beside me, looking at me with his intense eyes. Realizing I hadn't introduced him around yet, I quickly did so.

"Good to meet you, man," Jason said, reaching out to shake his hand. "I'm a big fan."

"Really?" Oliver gave Jason's Mr. Prep outfit a once-over, looking a bit skeptical.

"Trust me, he is," Teresa assured him,

rolling her eyes. "He's made me listen to that 'Brain Shock' song of yours at least a million times." Suddenly realizing what she'd said, she smiled sheepishly. "Not that I mind, of course. It's a cool song."

Oliver laughed. "Hey, I like this chick," he said to me, pointing at Teresa. "She speaks her mind. That's cool."

"Oh, look," Teresa said, clearly fishing for a change of topic. "Andy just came in. Andy! Over here!"

Sure enough, my favorite ex had just walked into the yard. Andy looked as cute as ever as he came over and joined us. But again I didn't pay nearly as much attention to that as I normally would have. Having Oliver there with me was even better than I'd expected. It was nice to be the center of attention again. That sort of thing had been sorely lacking in my life since Camzilla got engaged.

"Hey, dude." Rocco greeted Andy with a complicated high-five routine. "How's it hanging? Haven't seen you in ages."

Andy ran a hand through his sandy hair to push it out of his eyes. "I'm just home for a couple weeks," he said. "I ran into Ava's dad at the club and he invited me to this party."

"The club, eh?" Oliver spoke up, slinging an arm around my shoulders and grinning down at me. "How very Main Line."

Andy blinked at him as if noticing him for the first time. "Uh, hello," he said. "I'm Andy."

"This is Oliver," I said. I glanced up at my date, trying not to shiver with glee at the feel of his arm around me. "Andy and I went to high school together."

Was it my imagination, or did a shadow of hurt pass over Andy's face? I wasn't sure. If it was there, it disappeared just as quickly as it had come.

"Oliver's a singer," Rocco told Andy. "He's with that band the Manayunk Mucus."

Oliver had let his messenger bag drop to the floor at his feet. While the others started talking about the local music scene, I grabbed the bag and slipped away to stash it in the pool house so it wouldn't end up a pool toy for my bratty cousins. By the time I returned, the conversation had turned from music back to the ever-present subject of the wedding. I returned to my place beside Oliver and he put his arm around me again, this time looping it around my waist.

Eventually the conversation turned to

Teresa's upcoming trip, then to sports, then to Andy's first year at college, then to some TV show the guys had all watched. After that Jason started talking about some comedy group he planned to go see soon, but by then I wasn't really listening that closely. I was much more focused on Oliver's hand. It had started out resting on my waist. But as we stood there, his fingers started wriggling around, playing with the waistband of my shorts and then slipping down my hip.

I didn't particularly mind the sensation. Then again, I was pretty sure my parents would be somewhat less than thrilled if they happened to see.

"Excuse us," I said to the group. I reached down and disentangled Oliver's hand from my shorts, holding it firmly in my own. "It's hot out here—I could use a drink. Want to come along, Oliver?"

He came willingly. "Your friends are pretty cool," he commented as we wandered toward the bar hand in hand.

"Yeah," I said. "I just wish Teresa wasn't going away. The wedding won't be the same without her."

"Oh, yeah?" He spun me around so we were facing each other. "Well, I don't wish any such thing, I'm afraid. See, with her out of the picture that means I'll have you all to myself."

I might have forgotten to breathe as I stared up at him. We were at the far corner of the pool area, halfway between the gate into the yard and the bar set up at the back corner. The artful little cascade of rocks at that end of the pool hid us from much of the rest of the yard, making it feel like a private moment despite all the commotion of the party.

Oliver dropped one of my hands and touched my chin with his long fingers. "I'm really glad you came to my show the other night, Ava Hamilton," he said in a low, husky voice.

I let my eyes flutter shut as he moved in for a kiss—a real one this time, not a peck on the cheek or forehead. His breath smelled faintly of cigarette smoke, but I didn't mind. One of his hands was still on my chin, and the other wrapped around my waist as he pulled me close. My own hands slid up around the back of his neck. I wondered if he could feel my heart pounding through my bikini top as I melted into the kiss.

When he pulled back, I was smiling. I opened my eyes. "That was . . ."

My voice trailed off as I noticed Lance standing a few feet away, staring at us. Oops! He'd obviously come into the yard—alone—just in time to witness our kiss. What were the odds? I hid my smile in Oliver's shoulder.

"Lance!" Camille hurried toward him from the other direction. "I'm so glad you came after all. I—"

She stopped short, belatedly coming into view of Oliver and me still standing there with our arms wrapped around each other. For a moment she just stood there staring. Then she grabbed Lance by the arm and dragged him off out of sight.

"What was that?" Oliver asked, glancing over his shoulder.

"Nothing," I assured him. "Nothing at all."

We got our drinks and returned to the party. The sun was beginning to sink toward the horizon, but the weather was getting warmer and stuffier by the moment, and a few adults were starting to join the little kids in the pool. When we rejoined Teresa and the others, Rocco and Jason were debating whether or not to jump in for a swim.

"How about it, Oliver?" Jason said, turning to us. "You up for a friendly game of water polo?"

"Not me, mate." Oliver glanced down at me. "Actually, I may slip out for a smoke. Where'd you put my bag, darlin'?"

Before I could answer, a shriek went up from the direction of the back door. When I looked that way, I saw Camille clutching a phone and looking distraught.

"Uh-oh," I said. "Looks like Bridezilla crisis 9,264 has begun. I'd better go see what's up."

Teresa came along as I hurried toward Camille. Oliver trailed along behind us.

"What's going on?" I asked my aunt Hazel, who was standing nearby, along with an elderly neighbor lady and another older woman I didn't know. Fortunately, Lance was nowhere in sight.

Aunt Hazel fluttered her hands. She's a fluttery type of person at the best of times, and with Camille moaning and gnashing her teeth—well, practically—she looked as if she might take flight at any moment.

"The woman on the phone just asked for Camille," she said. "I didn't think to ask if it was something that might disrupt the party."

"There, there, dear." The neighbor lady patted her on the arm, then looked at me.

"It seems one of the flower girls can't make it to the wedding."

"Chicken pox? *Chicken pox?*" Camille cried, tossing the phone onto a chair. "Are you *kidding* me? Kids are all vaccinated against that these days! Who gets chicken pox anymore?"

"The Bakers just moved back from Hong Kong," Aunt Hazel reminded her soothingly. "I guess they don't vaccinate for that over there, maybe?"

Camille looked ready to cry. Aunt Hazel shot me a helpless glance. I traded a shrug with Teresa and then glanced around for Mom—she could defuse this crisis if anyone could. But she was nowhere to be seen.

"Babe?" Oliver tugged on my arm. "My bag. Really, I could use a ciggy. Where'd you put it?"

"Um, I stuck it in the pool house." I waved vaguely toward the little building.

"Cool." He hurried off without another word, looking relieved.

I wasn't thrilled that my new man was apparently so addicted to his gross little habit. But at the moment it was the least of my concerns.

"Listen, Camille," I said. "Believe it or not, this isn't a huge deal. It's not like Brittany Baker was your only flower girl. The others will just have to pick up the slack."

"What?" She looked as scandalized as if I'd suggested she walk down the aisle naked. "But there have to be *three* flower girls! It will look totally lame if there's an even number—everyone knows that!"

My brain hadn't quite finished processing that ridiculous proclamation when there came a piercing scream from the direction of the pool house. Everyone at the party stopped short and turned to look.

"Oh, dear," Aunt Hazel fluttered. "What was—"

At that moment someone came shooting out of the pool house. It was Oliver. He was clutching his bag and streaking for the exit, as wide-eyed and pale-faced as if he'd seen a ghost.

"Hey," I called out to him. "Oliver, wait . . ."

I didn't bother to continue. He was already gone.

"Wow," Teresa commented. "Guess he *really* needs that smoke."

Meanwhile, everyone else was buzzing about the scream. A moment later my mother stepped out of the pool house. She was wearing her tasteful Talbots bathing suit, a pair of slides, and a sheepish smile. As usual she looked great.

"It's all right, everyone," she called out. "Sorry if I startled you with that scream. Now, where did that young man go? I'm afraid I just scared him half to death. He walked in while I was changing."

Several people shouted with laughter, while others giggled a bit more discreetly. I could feel my face going several shades of red. So much for my supercool date . . .

I hurried over to Mom. "Uh—what?" was all I could manage.

Somehow, getting caught *in flagrante naked-o* appeared to have made Mom relax more than she had all day. Maybe she'd just needed a good laugh to loosen her up.

"Sorry about your date, Ava," she said with an amused smile. "I hope he's not too traumatized. I know I haven't been to the gym quite enough lately. . . ." She ran a hand over her perfectly toned tummy.

"Nonsense, Jane!" A woman from Mom's gardening club was standing close enough to hear her. "That was probably the best view he's had all week." She tittered behind her hand.

Several others heard the remark and laughed as well. Jason was among them.

"Nice date, Ava," he said, strolling over to join Teresa and me. "You invite him to this lovely party and he repays you by doing a Peeping Tom on your mom. What a perv."

"Very funny," I muttered. Okay, so maybe Oliver hadn't handled things too well just now. Did that mean Jason had to rub it in?

He kept grinning. I could tell he was thoroughly enjoying this. "It's a good thing the gate was open," he added. "Otherwise he would've left an Oliver-shaped hole in it, like in a Road Runner cartoon."

Teresa smiled wryly. "He *did* look pretty spooked, Ave. I'm guessing we might not see him again today."

"Yeah," Jason said. "He's probably halfway back to Philly by now. On foot."

I sighed, not bothering to respond. It didn't matter, anyway—Jason would just keep on making jokes until he ran out. Glancing over, I saw that Mom had already spotted Camille's distressed face and gone to see what was wrong. A few people still appeared to be laughing over the Oliver incident, but Mom gave no indication that she was paying them any attention at all. She already seemed to be over it, and I decided that the best thing to do was follow her lead.

It didn't matter, anyway. By the following Saturday nobody would even remember this. It wouldn't have any effect at all on the great time Oliver and I were going to have at the wedding.

Eleven

By Tuesday I was starting to get frantic. Oliver still hadn't returned any of my calls, even though I'd left at least fifteen messages on his voice mail and sent him three or four e-mails just in case there was a problem with his phone. What was going on?

I was so distracted at work that day that I accidentally filed half the new shipment of Burpee seed packets in the Seeds of Change slots. "Please, Ava," Mr. Baum said, looking slightly pained as he grabbed a misplaced packet of watermelon seeds. "Remember, your time off doesn't start until the end of your shift."

"I know. Sorry, Mr. B." I started putting the watermelons and the rest of the seeds where they belonged as he hurried off toward the registers.

When I'd finished unpacking the rest of the shipment, I checked my watch. Just an hour to go, and then I was off until after the wedding.

My phone rang. I grabbed it out of my apron pocket and checked the return number. Then I let out a gasp.

"Oliver?" I cried into the phone. "Where have you been? I've been trying to reach you for the past two days!"

"Sorry about that, babe." His husky voice was nonchalant. "Been kinda busy. The band got a call to come up to New York for a couple of gigs this weekend. Had to drop everything and hop a train."

"Wait—what?" I was still so surprised that he'd finally called back that my brain was having trouble keeping up. "You mean this weekend as in *this* weekend? As in the weekend you're supposed to be going to this wedding with me?"

"Yeah, that's sort of why I'm calling. Gotta bail on that one—hope you aren't mad."

No. My mind refused to accept this. He couldn't be backing out of our date *four days* before the wedding. It just wasn't possible.

But it was. By the time I hung up I was in full Camille-worthy panic mode. After glancing around to make sure Mr. Baum was nowhere in sight, I ducked behind a display of hose nozzles and called Teresa.

". . . and so now I have *four days* to find a new date," I finished with a gasp. I'd blurted out the entire story without taking a breath. "Actually, less than that. Tuesday's half over already. And the rehearsal dinner is Friday night."

"Yeah." Teresa sounded a little distracted. "Listen, I'm on my way to the barn. But think about this, Ava. Is the universe trying to tell you something? Like, maybe you should just give up on the perfect date thing and go by yourself? You've been so obsessive about this that Jason's starting to call you Camille Junior."

"Bite your tongue!" I said. "I'm nothing like Camille. Since when does Jason know anything about me, anyway?"

"Whatever. We can psychoanalyze you later. Just think about what I said."

She hung up. I frowned down at my phone for a moment, annoyed by her comment. Or rather Jason's comment.

Deciding I didn't have time to worry

about it, I hurried to the back room and reached into my bag for my unblack book. Then I sat down on a folding chair and started dialing.

I reached deep into the book. *Deep.* As in guys-I-hadn't-talked-to-in-years deep. Fifth-grade-summer-camp deep. Still no luck. Maybe Teresa was right. Maybe it was fate that I go to this wedding on my own. The universe certainly seemed to be conspiring pretty hard against me. . . .

Then I stopped short as a beautiful idea hit me. A beautiful, gorgeous, well-built idea with shoulders made to fill a tux and abs to die for.

"Ava?" Tommy stuck his head into the back room. "Mr. Baum is looking for you. Something about the orchids?"

I groaned. I'd promised to rearrange the orchid display so the plants with the best blooms were up front to tempt the customers. Normally I liked doing that sort of thing—it certainly beat stacking heavy bags of potting soil. But today it was just another obstacle in my quest for a new wedding date.

"Tell him I'm taking care of it right now," I said, standing up and hurrying out.

As I shifted the dendrobiums and cattleyas around on their mesh table with one hand, I dialed Rocco's number with the other. I hadn't paid that much attention to him at the pool party, since I hadn't thought it mattered, but I couldn't remember him mentioning going to the wedding. I crossed my fingers as the phone started to ring.

The universe was with me this time. Nobody had asked him yet.

"You're on, Ava," he said, sounding pleased. "It should be fun. And hey, while we're at it, why don't we get together tomorrow night? You know, get a little better acquainted, figure out what I should wear . . ."

"Perfect," I said. "How about dinner at that new Italian place in Bryn Mawr?"

"I'll pick you up at eight."

I was smiling when I hung up. Why hadn't I thought of Rocco sooner? It would have saved me a lot of trouble and anxiety. I had no expectations of True Love at this point; all I needed was a congenial date to fill out the tux. Rocco was perfect for that. He was a friendly guy with a terrific sense of humor, and there was no question that he would cut an impressive figure in formal attire. I was sure the two of us would have a fantastic, friendly time. All the other girls would be drooling over him, and I'd still have plenty of freedom to flirt my heart out with Andy and/or Kwan.

My phone was still in my hand as I reached over to pluck an old blossom off a phalaenopsis. I thought about calling Teresa to gloat, but decided it could wait—she usually turned her phone off while she was at the barn anyway.

Just then the phone rang in my hand. My heart stopped; for a second I was certain that it was Rocco calling me back to say he'd just been run over by a bus or something and couldn't make it.

But when I checked the number, my aortas and ventricles started pumping again immediately. It was only Camille.

"What is it this time?" I asked without preamble.

"Ava? Is that you?"

I rolled my eyes. "No, this is the mugger who stole Ava's phone."

"This is no time for jokes, Ava." Camille sounded testy—what else was new? "This is an emergency!"

I held the phone out from my ear a few

inches as she launched into one of her patented Bridezilla rants. Her shrill voice poured out of the tiny speaker, shattering the peace of the quiet greenhouse. A couple of passing customers gave me funny looks, but I just smiled at them as if everything were normal.

When Camille finally stopped for a breath, I returned the phone to my ear. "Let me get this straight," I said. "You're freaking out because the caterers got the wrong kind of *olives?* Who even notices olives?"

"I do!" she cried. "And for all the money Daddy is paying them, you'd think they could get it right! But they simply refuse to make this good; they claim there's not enough time to order the other kind, and Mom refuses to drive into Philadelphia with me to look for them, and Bob won't have time after work . . ."

Normally in this sort of situation I would have pretended to get another call and then passed Camille off to my mother or the wedding planner. But thanks to the resolution of my latest date crisis, I was feeling generous.

"Listen," I said. "I have an idea. The other day at the party, Jason was saying something about driving into Philly to see some comedy show in the park. I *think* it was some afternoon this week." I paused, trying to remember back. The details were vague—Jason's social plans certainly hadn't been my top priority that day—but I was pretty sure I had the important parts right. "I can call him and see when he's going. Maybe he'd be willing to swing by the Italian Market and see what he can find."

"Oh, my God! Do you think he'd really do that?" Camille sounded pathetically grateful. "That would be totally amazing!"

She gave me the olive 411, insisting that I write everything down so I wouldn't mess it up. I jotted the notes on the Post-it pad in my apron pocket, then hung up and called Jason.

He listened quietly while I gave him the scoop. "So you want me to go look for these olives?" he said.

"Could you?" I put a little wheedle into my voice. "I mean, if your comedy thing is sometime in the next couple of days, that is . . ."

"It's today, actually," he said. "The show starts at four."

I checked my watch. It was twenty

minutes to one. "Perfect!" I exclaimed. I turned up the wheedle a little more. "If you wanted to leave a little early, you could swing by the Italian Market first and then head over to the park from there."

"I suppose I could," he said. "But what if I can't find the right olives? I think maybe you'd better come along."

That one I hadn't been expecting. The only thing worse than spending a beautiful afternoon on some pointless Bridezilla errand was doing the same with annoying Jason, and I would've thought he would feel the same way about me. Then again, I supposed I should be grateful he'd even consider helping out. . . .

"Um, I'm at work," I said, hoping that might be enough to get me out of it.

I should have known better. "What time do you get off?" he asked.

Cursing my parents for teaching me that lying was wrong, I said weakly, "One o'clock."

"Perfect. I'll be waiting."

Before I could say anything else, he hung up. I glared at the phone in my hand. Then, tucking it back into my pocket, I decided I might as well look on the bright side. At least this errand would keep me away from home—and Camille's "emergencies"—for a few hours. I called my mom to tell her the plan. Then I threw myself back into my work, vowing to use that last twenty minutes to make up for my earlier slacking.

True to his word, Jason was parked in the loading zone outside the store when I walked out with a coworker named Gina, who was heading out for her lunch break. As we got closer, he leaned over from the driver's seat to open the passenger side door.

"Your chauffeur awaits," he said.

Gina elbowed me. "Oh my God—is that the new guy?" she asked in a loud stage whisper. "He's adorable!"

I realized she must think Jason was Zoom—I'd mentioned him to her one day when we'd had lunch together and hadn't had a chance to update her. "Not exactly," I said, wondering if Jason had heard. I said good-bye to Gina and hopped into the car, not meeting Jason's eye. "Thanks, Jeeves. Drive on."

I flashed back to the last time I'd been alone in his car with him, when he'd driven me to work after my first and only date with

Zoom. It had felt weird not to have Teresa there then, and it felt even weirder now. After all, that time had been nothing more than a chance encounter. This time we were together, well, *on purpose*. Weird.

We were both quiet for a few minutes as Jason drove to the exit. Since it was around lunchtime, traffic was heavy on Route 30, with hot, cranky drivers leaning on their horns every time the lights changed color. Finally Jason saw his chance and scooted out to join the flow heading east.

"So," I said, searching for a topic that might get us past the awkwardness. "Since you made me come along, I guess I'm stuck going to this comedy thing, too. So what is it, exactly?"

"My friend Bonner's improv comedy troupe. They're putting on a charity show in Fairmount Park."

"What charity?"

"A few different ones, actually—all environmental stuff." He glanced over at me. "You're into that sort of thing, right? Teresa said you did your senior volunteer project on alternative energy."

It felt weird that he knew something like that about me. "Uh-huh," I said. "So are you into that sort of thing, too, or are you just looking for a few laughs?"

He shrugged, easing to a stop at a red light. "Well, I'm hoping to specialize in environmental law someday. Does that count?"

I laughed sheepishly. "Really? I didn't know that."

In some corner of my mind I vaguely remembered Teresa mentioning that Jason wanted to go to law school after college. At the time I'd probably made some snide comment about how he was perfectly cut out to join one of those ambulance-chasing firms that advertised on late-night TV. After what he'd just said, I felt a bit guilty. Maybe he wasn't quite as shallow as I'd always thought.

"Did you have lunch yet?"

I blinked, startled out of my thoughts by the abrupt question. "No," I replied. "Did you?"

He shook his head. "I've been craving a good cheesesteak all week. Want to swing by Pat's or somewhere? You're not one of those girls who only eats salad, are you?"

I shot him a surprised glance. I'd had enough meals with him and Teresa for him to know the answer to that question. Then I caught the twinkle in his eye and realized he was joking.

"I can eat a weenie-boy like you under the table anytime, anywhere," I joked back. "Bring it on!"

Before long we were standing on the heat-baked sidewalk outside Pat's King of Steaks in South Philly, doing our best to control the huge gobs of provolone and fried onion that were doing their best to slide out of our sandwiches. The exhaust fumes from the cars on Passyunk Avenue added an urban touch to the scents of sizzling steak and onions.

"This is the stuff," Jason said happily, slurping a blob of melted cheese off his hand.

"Totally," I agreed. I love a good cheesesteak, and it's always nice to see someone else enjoy one just as much. I was shocked to realize I was actually having a good time with Jason. Up until now he'd always been nothing more than a slightly annoying third wheel tagging along when I was hanging out with Teresa. The only times I'd really talked to him alone were when she was off in the bathroom or something.

I always thought he and I had nothing in common, I mused. *But now we've found agreement twice in one day—first there was the environmental thing, and now it turns out both of us prefer Pat's steaks over Geno's.* I glanced over at the competing cheesesteak place across the street, then back at Jason. *What are the odds?*

"Why are you looking at me like that?" he asked.

"Like what?" I blushed slightly, glad that he couldn't read my thoughts. "I'm not staring at you. I'm just enjoying my— what?" I said as I noticed him grinning at me in an odd way.

"You have cheese on your face."

"Oh. Thanks." I swiped at my cheek with a napkin, glad—and a little surprised, actually—that he hadn't just let me walk around like that all day.

"Other side," Jason said. I tried again, but he shook his head. "Hold still," he ordered.

He reached out and swept his thumb over my left cheekbone. I held my breath, hoping he didn't notice that I'd shivered at his touch. The worst part was, I had no idea why. After all, this was *Jason* we were talking about. My best friend's boyfriend, the most annoying guy in the tristate area, the bane of my existence. Why in the world would *his* touch make me tingle?

I turned away and chowed down on my sandwich to hide my confusion. Maybe it was true what Teresa always said: that I was boy crazy and could find the diamond in even the roughest guy. I'd always taken it as sort of a compliment. But if being boy crazy meant going gooey like melted cheese at even *Jason's* touch, I was ready to commit myself.

Then again, I'd had a rough couple of weeks, guy-wise. Maybe I needed to cut myself some slack.

"Almost ready?" I asked, taking one last bite of my steak before dumping the rest in the trash. "Let's go get those olives so Camille can take her head out of the oven."

"Okay. But we need to find a real parking spot first." The heart of the Italian Market was only a couple of blocks away from where we were standing. But the free lot on Kimball had been full when we'd cruised by, so Jason had just double-parked on the street near the steak places.

Parking in South Philly could be challenging at the best of times, but that day it was practically a comedy of errors. We were right behind the car that got the last available spot on Christian Street. We waited with the turn signal on for almost ten minutes while an old man slowly loaded bags into his trunk, only to realize that he wasn't actually leaving. We pulled into a beautiful space—but immediately realized it was a fire hydrant. We even drove the wrong way down a one-way street. By accident, of course. At least that's what Jason claimed after I screamed, closed my eyes, and clutched at the hand rest for dear life. When he did the same thing a second time, though, I couldn't help wondering.

"This is getting ridiculous," I said through clenched teeth as he spun around the same corner for the umpteenth time. "Why don't you just drop me off and drive around? I can dash in, find the olives, and wait for you to swing by again."

"Are you sure you trust me enough for that?" he asked with a grin. For some reason he didn't really seem bothered by the frustration of parking. Or rather *not* parking. "I might just drive off and abandon you."

"Oh, I trust you," I replied grimly.

"Because if you did that, I'd tell Teresa on you and she'd kick your butt."

He didn't seem to have an answer for that one, probably because he knew I was right. A moment later he leaned forward over the steering wheel. "There's one," he said.

Sure enough, a car had just pulled out half a block ahead. I held my breath, not daring to believe we might actually have found a viable parking place. What was going to stop us this time? Loading zone? Driveway? Prius-swallowing pothole?

A moment later Jason had neatly parallel parked in the spot. "There we go," he said cheerfully. "No problem."

I rolled my eyes. "Okay, let's get this over with," I said, unhooking my seat belt. "I've always liked that little place on the corner—what's it called? Talluto's? We should check there first."

"No, let's try DiBruno's," Jason argued. "They have everything."

"Fine, whatever." I wasn't in the mood to argue.

DiBruno's was packed, as usual, and we had to wait in line for fifteen minutes just for the chance to ask about the right olives. When we got to the front of the line, the clerk shrugged helplessly. They had about half a million kinds of olives, but not the kind Camille wanted.

"Sorry," Jason said sheepishly. "Guess we should've gone to your place after all."

"See? That just goes to show that you should always listen to me. Because I'm always right."

I was only joking, of course, but I still had to eat my words when Talluto's didn't have the right kind of olives either. "Sorry, *signora*," the cute old Mediterranean lady behind the counter said with a shrug. "Sold out."

"What now?" Jason asked as we went back outside.

"I don't know," I said, staring absently at the people wandering back and forth on the street. "But I don't want to imagine what Camille will say if I show up at home without those olives. Let's check around a little more."

We actually found the olives at the next place we tried. "Duh," Jason muttered as the clerk was ringing me up. "I should've remembered that Claudio's is the best place for olives."

"Thank you," I said to the clerk as he

handed me my receipt. "You just saved my life."

I glanced at my watch as we stepped back outside. My heart sank. Where had the time gone? It was already five after four. This errand had definitely taken a lot longer than expected.

"Oops," I said. "I guess your friend's comedy show already started. Sorry about that."

I braced myself for his annoyance or obnoxious teasing or both. I pretty much deserved it this time. Okay, so the parking problems hadn't been my fault, and it hadn't been my idea to stop for cheesesteaks, either. Still, I *had* been the one to beg him to follow my sister's latest crazy whim.

But he merely shrugged. "No biggie," he said. "I'll catch them next time."

"Really? You don't mind?" I was surprised. "But it sounded like you were really looking forward to it."

"It's okay. I had fun today anyway. What could be better than cheesesteaks and a beautiful afternoon at the Italian Market?"

I grinned. "This *was* kind of fun, I guess," I said, realizing it was true. "At least parts of it."

We got in the car and headed for home. Along the way, we chatted about this and that—almost like real friends. I even found myself laughing at most of his goofy jokes.

When we were just a few blocks from my house, I sighed. "Almost back to Planet Camille. For a while there I forgot that the world now revolves around veils and vows."

"And fancy olives, of course," Jason added.

I laughed. "How could I forget?" Feeling a sudden wave of fondness for him, I smiled down at the Claudio bag at my feet. For the first time I felt as if I could see a little of what Teresa saw in Jason. He really was a sweet guy under that perfect hair and class-clown attitude. "Thanks for distracting me from all that for a while, Jason." Impulsively I added, "You know, maybe it isn't the worst thing in the world that Teresa dragged you home. You're okay."

He didn't answer. When I glanced over, he was staring straight ahead with both hands gripping the wheel, even though we were driving on a quiet road. Had I embarrassed him? I hadn't thought such a thing was possible.

Deciding to take pity on him, I changed

the subject. "You know, after all this effort, the least Camille could do is invite you to the wedding. You've more than earned a helping of salmon and a little Macarena."

"That's okay." He suddenly turned to grin at me. "I was already planning to lurk around outside the wedding on Saturday to get some photos of you in your dress—the Pink Horror, didn't you call it? If you give me a flash of your SpongeBobs, I may even post it on my MySpace."

I sighed. So much for my warm, fuzzy feelings toward him; Mr. Obnoxious had returned. "Thanks for the ride," I said, grabbing the olives and sliding out of the car. "See you later."

Twelve

"Sure you don't want a drink, Ava?" Rocco asked as the waitress brought him his seventh beer. He was only eighteen, but with his impressive bulk and deep voice he could easily pass for twenty-one. The waitress hadn't even asked for ID when he'd ordered his first Corona.

I shook my head. "No thanks. I'm good."

The restaurant was still fairly busy even though it was getting late. Rocco and I had been there for more than two hours. We'd long since finished our food but had lingered, sharing a dessert and nursing our drinks—Rocco beer, me iced tea—while talking, laughing, reminiscing about high school, and generally having a great time.

Sometime around his third beer I'd been worried that Rocco might turn into one of those obnoxious drunks, like a lot of the other jocks from our school who closed out parties by breaking things or running down the street naked. But if anything each beer only seemed to make him sweeter and friendlier.

Finally, I glanced at my watch. "We should probably get going," I said, reluctant to end the evening but knowing I should. "I have a busy day tomorrow."

"Oh, really?" Rocco chugged part of his beer, then leaned closer across the table, knocking over the salt shaker as he grabbed my hand. "What are you doing, besides looking beautiful?"

I smiled to acknowledge the compliment. Drunken or not, that sort of thing was always nice to hear. Especially from a guy who could pass for Mr. Universe himself. If Rocco looked this good in jeans and a striped polo, I couldn't wait to see him all dressed up for the wedding.

"I'm under orders from Camille to go pick up the wedding favors in the morning," I said. "She's giving everyone these little engraved silver bells. Wedding bells—get it?"

"That sounds beautiful. Almost as beautiful as you."

Okay, he was a sweet drunk, but now he was turning into a repetitive one too. "Anyway," I continued, "Teresa's got her mom's car for the day, so she's going to drive me to get the stuff. Then we're going up to the mall to do some shopping and have lunch at the sushi place there. Sort of a final chance to hang out before she leaves for Germany the day after tomorrow."

I felt a pang at those last three words: "day after tomorrow." I couldn't believe Teresa was leaving so soon. I missed her already—between the wedding craziness and my own dating adventures, the last two weeks had flown by super fast. It almost felt as if I'd seen more of Jason than I had of her.

Rocco flagged down the waitress and paid the bill. A few minutes later we were walking out into the warm summer night. Well, *I* was walking. Rocco was staggering a little.

"I'm thinking you shouldn't drive," I told him. "Why don't we call a cab?"

"I have a better idea." He grinned and pressed his car keys into my hand. "Want to try out my new ride?"

"Really? Sure!" Rocco's parents had bought him a brand-new top-of-the-line BMW as a graduation gift. They could afford it now that they didn't have to pay for college—he'd landed himself a free ride to Penn State on a football scholarship.

It only took me a couple of minutes to get the hang of the Beemer. Luckily, Rocco just laughed when I ground the gears a few times—like I said, I didn't usually drive much.

Soon we were cruising down the avenue with the windows open. The night air rushed in, tossing my hair around in my face. There wasn't much traffic this late, so the usually busy road had an oddly intimate feel. Passing all the familiar Main Line landmarks, with an amazing old high-school buddy beside me, I felt a sudden rush of nostalgia. Soon I would be leaving all this behind for college. The adventurous part of me was looking forward to getting out into the world, meeting new people, trying new things. But another part of me was thinking that it was just too soon. Why couldn't everything stay the same for a little while longer?

"Hey." Rocco interrupted my thoughts, leaning closer and jabbing a finger at the windshield. "Let's go drive past the school."

"You mean our high school? Why?" I asked, wondering if he was thinking the same sorts of thoughts as I was. We were almost at the turnoff by now. I hit the turn signal and spun the wheel.

He shrugged. "Just thought it would be fun to check out the place at night," he rumbled, his voice even deeper than usual. "You know—for old times' sake."

Soon we were pulling into the familiar parking lot. The building loomed in front of us, looking somehow somber and strange in the dark, as if aware that it had already pushed us off into adulthood and shut us out.

"Why don't we stop over there for a few minutes?" Rocco pointed out a parking spot at the far end of the lot beneath several large, overhanging willows at the edge of the sports fields.

By now I had a pretty good idea of what he had in mind. Sure enough, when I turned off the car he immediately hopped out and hurried around the front of the car, only swaying a little. I unclipped my seat belt and opened my door.

"Come here, beautiful," he said in that extralow, throaty voice. He sounded sort of like Barry White, if Barry White were young and hot with abs of steel. Pulling me out of the car, Rocco wrapped his arms around me and kissed me.

I went limp, sinking into the embrace. He was an excellent kisser.

We moved over to the bench under the willow trees. He sat down and pulled me gently onto his lap. "This is nice," I murmured, pushing my hair out of the way.

"Uh-huh." His hand was so big that it cupped my entire head as he pulled me toward him again.

We made out for quite a while, and things got a bit hot and heavy. It wasn't until a car cruised past on the quiet street nearby with its radio blaring that I reluctantly decided I'd better get home. My parents weren't too strict about curfews and such, but even they might notice if I didn't wander in until two a.m.

I drove us home with his warm hand resting on my knee. We didn't talk much; I'm pretty sure he was starting to fall asleep. But I was wide awake. I hadn't been expecting much out of this evening other than a nice time with an old high-school friend. But if things continued on this way, I just might have to rethink that. . . .

I parked his car on the street halfway between our two homes. Then I stuck the keys in his pocket and gave him a shove in the direction of his house, watching him stagger off just long enough to feel reassured that he was going to make it the whole three blocks home without falling over. Then I turned and headed for my own house, enjoying the cool air and the quiet of the sleepy neighborhood.

"What are you smiling about?" Camille growled when I walked in. She and Mom were at the kitchen table poring over what looked like seating charts.

"Nothing." I smiled even wider. "Good night."

"Don't forget you have to pick up the favors tomorrow!" Camille yelled after me as I skipped toward the stairs.

The next morning I was still in a great mood. Not only was I going to have the best-looking date at the wedding, but after the previous evening I was actually getting a bit smitten with him. And based on the way he'd kissed me, I was pretty sure he felt the same. What could be better? This time I was sure all the drama had been worth it, now that I'd ended up with Rocco. I couldn't wait to tell Teresa all about it.

I was surprised and disappointed to see Jason's Prius pull into the driveway instead of Teresa's mother's black sedan. "What are you doing here?" I demanded as I hurried toward the car.

"Nice way to talk to a guy who's doing you a favor," Jason called back through the open window. "Come on, get in."

"Where's Teresa?" I climbed into the empty passenger seat, still a little confused.

He shrugged and put the car in gear. "Apparently she didn't know the people at the barn were throwing her a surprise bon voyage party this morning."

"Duh. That's what the word 'surprise' means, genius." It came out a little ruder than I'd meant it to, since I was genuinely disappointed that Teresa wasn't there.

Luckily, he didn't seem to notice. "Plus it turns out her mom needs the car today after all, so Teresa asked me to drive you out to Paoli to pick up the wedding stuff. Then I'll drop you off at the mall—she said she'll be there to meet you by eleven."

"Oh. Okay." I leaned back against the seat. My happy mood was already seeping back. "Um, thanks, by the way. Camille would kill me if I didn't pick up those favors." I giggled. "On the plus side, if I were dead, I wouldn't have to wear the Pink Horror. Well, unless she insisted I be buried in it—that's totally something Camille would do. And then I'd just have to come back and haunt the wedding, and it would be a big mess. . . ."

"You're welcome." He shot me a glance as he paused at a stop sign. "So what's with you, anyway? You're, like, extra weird today."

"Gee, thanks." I laughed, unable to work up even a little bit of annoyance at him today. "If you really want to know, I'm in love! Well—at least in *like*."

"Really?" He returned his gaze to the road as he turned the corner. "Who's the lucky guy?"

"Rocco. Remember? You met him at the pool party."

"Oh, right. Rocco the Jocko. Your latest wedding date."

He didn't sound particularly interested. Still, I couldn't resist continuing. "He's this total football stud, incredibly gorgeous . . ." I let out a happy sigh. "We went out last night and had such a good time."

I paused, waiting for the teasing to start. For once I didn't even mind. After spending so much time with Jason lately, I was starting to feel almost fond of him.

But Jason remained silent. He didn't even look over at me.

"Well?" I prompted. "Aren't you going to make one of your snotty comments? Like, that I'd fall for a turnip if it had a cute butt? Anything? Anything? Bueller?"

He finally glanced over. "Oh," he said. "You mean a comment like, say, you have more dates than a Middle Eastern market?"

I groaned. "Oh, please," I teased. "You can do better than that. Come on—I have faith in you."

"Fine." He sped up to make it through a yellow light. "Maybe I should say that they're thinking of putting your picture next to the word 'fickle' in the dictionary."

"Ouch," I said, annoyance breaking through my sunny mood at last. That one had been a little harsher than his usual type of comment.

"Didn't like that one, hmm? How about this one—your phone number is probably on every men's room wall between here and New Jersey."

"Hey." My giddy mood deflated like a child's inflatable toy popped by a needle. A big, mean, obnoxious needle. Here I'd been expecting his usual goofy, SpongeBob-level teasing, and he was basically calling me a slut. "You don't have to be rude about it."

"Whatever," he growled.

There was a moment of tense silence in the car. It was interrupted by my cell phone going off.

I grabbed it out of my purse. "Hello?"

"Ava? I'm glad I reached you." There was no mistaking Rocco's deep, rumbling voice.

"Rocco!" I smiled, tossing Jason a triumphant look. "What's up?"

"I need to see you," he said, sounding kind of urgent. "Right away. It's important."

"Really? You need to see me again?" I lifted one eyebrow slightly and shot another glance across the car. "Well, I'm going to King of Prussia to meet Teresa for lunch. Maybe we can meet up afterward?"

"Um, okay, I guess," he mumbled.

"I'll give you a call. Bye." I hung up and tucked my phone away. "Well," I said to the car at large. "I guess *some* people don't think I'm so fickle."

He didn't answer. I rolled my eyes. Obviously the tolerable time I'd had with him in South Philly had been a fluke. I must have been crazy to think it was a good thing Teresa had brought him home. At the moment I was more than ready for her to dump him and get him out of both our lives.

Thirteen

"I can't believe you're leaving tomorrow," I said for about the fifteenth time.

Teresa glanced at her watch. "Nineteen hours and counting."

We were at our favorite sushi place at the mall. I'd arrived to find Teresa waiting for me outside of Neiman Marcus, where her mom had just dropped her off. It had been a relief to see her, especially after the last part of the drive with Jason. We'd barely said a word to each other while running Camille's errand or on the ride up to the mall afterward. I was annoyed with him over what he'd said, and I could tell he was annoyed at me, too, though I had no idea why. I certainly hadn't called *him* a slut.

When he had pulled over to the curb, I'd expected him to try to horn in on our girls' time by inviting himself along. That was the type of thing he always did, and today it would've had the bonus of getting back at me for whatever he thought I'd done or said. But he'd barely slowed down long enough for me to get out before peeling out again with just a quick wave to Teresa. I only hoped he'd remember to drop off the favors at my house as promised.

I didn't worry about his behavior for long, though. After all, with Teresa away I wasn't going to have to see Jason for at least a month. Besides, I wasn't about to let him ruin my last day with Teresa before her trip. We spent a while picking up a few last-minute things she needed, then headed to the sushi place for lunch.

"But enough about my trip." Teresa grabbed a piece of yellowtail with her chopsticks. "Tell me more about your date. I can't believe you and Rocco made out!"

"I know." I shivered as I thought back. "It was amazing. You know how some guys are kind of, you know, selfish kissers?" For a second I flashed to an image of her and Jason making out. Not that I'd ever seen them do more than trade a good-bye peck on the lips—Teresa was private that way. "Um, anyway," I continued, a little flustered. Why was I still wasting time thinking about Jason? "Rocco isn't like that. He's totally tender, and would sort of wait for me to take the lead sometimes, and . . ."

I trailed off as I noticed that Teresa was staring over my shoulder toward the restaurant entrance. "Here's Hot Lips now," she said.

"What?" I turned around in my seat. Sure enough, Rocco had just entered. His bulk practically filled the doorway as he stood there looking around. He was wearing a Nittany Lions T-shirt and an anxious expression.

Then he spotted me. He waved to me, looking downright frantic now.

"Wow," I said, putting down my chopsticks. "He seemed kind of eager to see me again, but this . . ."

Rocco moved surprisingly fast for such a big guy. He dodged between the tables and was at ours in seconds flat.

"Ava," he rumbled breathlessly. "I was hoping I'd find you here."

I wavered between being incredibly flattered and a tiny bit annoyed. "Um, I thought we were going to do something later," I said. "Teresa and I—"

He barely glanced at Teresa before stepping closer and reaching for my hand. "I'm sorry, but I just couldn't wait until later," he announced. "I had to talk to you *now*."

His deep voice was never particularly quiet, but it was rising dramatically with every word. I winced as people all over the quiet restaurant glanced our way in surprise.

"What is it?" I hissed, as if talking more quietly myself might give him the hint.

It didn't. "There's something I've never told anyone before," he said, clutching my hand so tightly that it started to throb a little. "Something important that I wasn't sure I was ready to handle."

"Uh-huh." I was barely listening, all too aware that more eyes were on us with every word. I wasn't the shy and retiring type, but it was still a bit embarrassing to have a guy about to loudly declare his love for me in front of a roomful of lunching ladies and hungry shoppers. Not to mention Teresa, who was still eating her sashimi and looking on with interest.

Rocco took a deep breath, dropped my hand, and straightened up to his full, impressive height. "Here goes," he said. "I'm—gay."

I blinked. Whatever I'd been expecting him to say, that wasn't it. "Um—huh—what?" I burbled, waiting for the punchline.

"I'm gay," he said again, then smiled. "Whew! That wasn't as bad as I thought. I'm gay. I'm gay!"

All around us, people were chuckling. The twentysomething couple at the next table started to clap, and within seconds the entire restaurant was applauding.

Rocco grinned, looking sheepish as he glanced around. "Thanks," he said. "Sorry to interrupt your meals."

"No problem, young man!" a dapper older gentleman at the sushi bar called out. He raised his glass in Rocco's direction. "Welcome to the tribe."

"Wow," Teresa said mildly. "That's big news, Rocco. I had no idea."

"Nobody did, I guess." He took a deep breath. "I'm going to tell my folks next. But I wanted to let Ava know first, since she was the one who—well, you know—helped me realize it."

"I did?" I was still stunned. Rocco the Jocko—gay? Okay, maybe there were a few little hints. Like the way he'd never seriously dated anyone in high school. Or the sweet, tender, caring way he'd kissed me last night . . . "Wait," I blurted out. "You mean you realized it, um—when we, you know . . ."

He pulled out one of the empty chairs at our table and perched on the edge of it, gazing at me earnestly. "I've been coming to terms with this for a long time now," he said. "I just maybe wasn't ready to accept it, you know? But when I kissed you last night, I finally had to face up to it. I was just trying too hard to be someone I'm not." He shrugged his massive shoulders. "And then I just felt too guilty hiding the truth from you—and the rest of the world—for one moment longer." He glanced at Teresa again. "Sorry to mess up your good-bye lunch, T."

"Don't worry about it." Teresa stood up and hurried around to give him a hug. "We totally understand. Right, Ava?"

"Right," I said blankly. Oh, well. So much for more of those great make-out sessions.

But I did my best to shrug off the twinges of disappointment. This wasn't about me. Besides, it was really no big deal. In fact, in a lot of ways a hot gay date was even better than the alternative. He was sure to arrive perfectly groomed and look great in the pictures, plus I wouldn't have to worry at all about hurting his feelings by flirting with other guys.

Realizing that Rocco was still staring at me with concern, I smiled reassuringly. "I'm glad you told me," I said, taking my turn at hugging him. "I know it must have been hard for you. But don't worry, you're such a great guy—I'm sure everyone will be really supportive when you tell them."

"I hope so." He looked relieved. "Thanks for being so understanding, Ava."

"No problem," I said, stepping back and sitting down again. "Just let me know if you want me to keep quiet about it for now or what. You know, on Saturday."

"Saturday?" The look of worry returned. "Oh—but I thought you understood. I can't go to the wedding with you."

"What?" I'd been reaching for my water glass, but now my hand froze in midair. "What do you mean, you can't go?"

He'd sat down again too, but now he stood up, gazing down at me from his full height. His face was sorrowful. "That's why I didn't want to wait to tell you. I hate to disappoint you, Ava, especially after you've been so good to me. But I can't go to that wedding with you." He put a hand to his heart dramatically. "Now that I finally know who I am, it would be like purposely living a lie!"

"No, it wouldn't," I argued, feeling desperate. "Anyway, it would only be living a lie for two more days."

"I'm sorry, Ava," he rumbled. "I can't do it for two more days. I couldn't even do it for two more seconds! I'm really sorry. I'll leave you guys alone now."

He turned and rushed off. "Rocco, wait!" I called.

But it was no use. He was gone.

I turned to stare at Teresa. "The wedding is the day after tomorrow," I exclaimed. "*Now* what am I supposed to do?"

Fourteen

I was tempted to call Rocco after he left and beg him to change his mind about going to the wedding. But Teresa quickly talked me out of it.

"He's going through a rough thing right now," she reminded me as we left the sushi place and sat down on a bench in the mall aisle. "This is bigger than some stupid wedding date. Leave him alone."

"Yeah, you're right." I sighed. "Okay, then help me figure out who else is left to call."

"You could just—"

"Don't say it!" I interrupted warningly. "I know I could go stag. But I don't want to, okay?"

She shrugged. I could tell she thought I was being ridiculous, but she was friend enough not to say so.

To be honest I wasn't even sure why I was being so stubborn about it. Maybe it was pride. It would be one thing if I'd decided to go alone on purpose. But at this point it would be more like giving up. And I didn't do that easily.

We talked it over as we headed outside to wait for Jason to pick us up. But it was hopeless. Every guy we knew already had a date.

"There's not even enough time to try to pick up someone new like I did with Zoom and Oliver," I moaned, flopping down on the sun-warmed curb.

"Besides, with your luck lately, whoever you found would probably get diagnosed with the bubonic plague twenty minutes before the wedding," Teresa commented.

I squinted up at her. "You're not helping."

"Sorry." She shrugged, setting down her shopping bags and checking her watch. "Jason should be here soon. Maybe he'll have some ideas." She smiled. "After all, he wants every other guy in a ten-mile radius to be at that wedding so he'll have

Burrito Moe's all to himself, remember?"

"Yeah, right." I knew she was just trying to cheer me up. But I certainly wasn't going to leave my social fate in Jason's hands, especially after his behavior earlier. "Hey, speak of the devil," I added as I saw a blue Prius heading our way.

"Hi," he said to Teresa as we climbed in. "What's with her?"

I guess my gloomy face had given me away. "None of your business," I said at the same time as Teresa replied, "Rocco's gay."

"Huh?" Jason said.

Despite my protests, Teresa quickly filled him in. She made him promise not to tell anybody else, though I'm not sure why, considering it was already old news to an entire restaurant full of people. "So now Ava's dateless again," she finished.

I waited for the joke, but Jason just shrugged. "Bummer," he muttered.

We didn't talk much on the ride to Teresa's father's office in Radnor. Jason was dropping her off there to meet her dad for a few more errands, then driving me home afterward. I wasn't relishing the thought of being alone with him again, but I forgot all about that as we arrived in the parking lot of the office complex and Teresa got out of the car. This was good-bye—I knew she and Jason had dinner plans that evening, and then she was leaving early the next morning to be at the airport in time for her connecting flight to New York.

I hopped out of the car, all thoughts of Jason, the wedding, and everything else seeming inconsequential for the moment. "I can't believe you're really leaving!" I cried, throwing my arms around her.

She hugged me back tightly. "I know," she said, her voice muffled by my hair. "It's crazy, right? Me—in Germany."

"You'll do great." I pulled back, keeping my hands on her arms as I gazed at her fondly. "But I'm going to miss you like crazy. E-mail me every day, okay? And send lots of postcards!"

"I promise." She hugged me again. "See you when I get home."

"You can count on it." After one last squeeze I reluctantly let her go. Jason was still in the car, his arm resting on the frame of the open window. He waved at Teresa. "I'll pick you up later," he called to her. Then he glanced at me. "All aboard. This train is leaving the station."

"I'm coming." Blowing one last kiss to Teresa, I got back into the backseat.

"You could sit up front, you know," he said, sounding almost hostile.

"No, thanks. This is fine." In truth I'd climbed into the back automatically. If he'd turned it into a joke and called me a ditz, I probably would have laughed it off and switched to the front. But if he was going to be a jerk about it, two could play that game.

"Whatever," he muttered, jamming the car back into drive and pulling away.

As we sped along toward home I slumped in my seat, running over my options—or lack thereof—in my head. There just didn't seem to be a good solution, unless I wanted to try trolling the local under-fourteen crowd for a date. Which I didn't.

Why did Lance have to do this to me? I thought. *I wish I'd told him off when he came to the store the other day.*

I blinked and sat up so fast that my seat belt almost cut off circulation in my stomach. "Hey, wait," I blurted out. "That's it!"

I smiled, suddenly sure that I'd found the perfect solution at last. Maybe I hadn't fully appreciated what I'd had with Lance. But if he was willing to seek me out to talk about it, maybe there was still a chance for us.

"What's it?" Jason glanced at me in the rearview. He still sounded kind of gruff and unfriendly, but I hardly noticed.

"Listen, Jason." I leaned forward and grabbed his shoulder. "Can you do me a huge favor? Drive me over to McNeilly's Garage."

"You mean now? Why?"

"I've got to talk to Lance, and it can't wait." I was talking fast now, certain that I'd finally found the answer. "See, he came to the store the other day while I was working. And he showed up at the pool party alone too. Why else would he do that if he wasn't hoping to rekindle things with me?"

"Wait, you want to talk to that Lance jerk?" Jason sounded a little more like his normal self. "Ava, I'm not sure that's a good idea."

"It's a great idea," I insisted. "He probably regrets breaking up with me. And if he does, he'd probably be thrilled if I told him we could still go to the wedding together!"

I could already imagine the delicious look of surprise on Lance's face when I turned up at his work just like he'd turned up at mine. And that surprise would turn to joy when he realized why I was there. . . .

Jason glanced back at me, biting his lip. "Are you sure you want to do this?" he asked. "That Lance guy was never good enough for you anyway."

"Look, are you willing to help me out or not?" I was practically bouncing up and down by now. "Because if you're not, just take me home and I'll find another ride."

He sighed. "No, it's okay. I'll take you."

I kept busy for the rest of the short ride practicing in my head what I was going to say. When Jason pulled into the parking lot of the garage, I spotted Lance immediately. He was standing at the edge of one of the bays, in front of a car raised a few feet up on a lift, talking to the pair of overall-clad legs sticking out from beneath it.

"I'll be right back," I told Jason. Then I got out and tiptoed over to Lance. His back was to me. The mechanic under the car was clanking and banging on something down there, and a radio was blasting reggae from the office nearby, so he didn't hear me coming. I reached out and clapped my hands over his eyes.

"Hey!" he cried.

"Surprise!" I sang out as he spun around. "Guess who?"

"Oh. Ava," he said uncertainly. Lance was never too quick on the uptake, so I figured it would take him a while to puzzle out why I was there.

I decided to take mercy on him and end the suspense without any playing around. After all, he was always most comfortable with the straightforward and obvious. That was one of his best qualities—no games.

"I need to talk to you, Lance," I said, raising my voice a little to make sure he could hear me above the reggae. So what if his buddy under the car overheard? At this point I didn't care if the entire Main Line heard what I had to say to him. "I've been thinking about us. You know—how things ended. It really seems like a shame to throw away three great months just like that."

"Ava, I—" he began.

I reached out and touched a finger to his lips. "Wait," I cut him off. "Just let me say this, okay? I think you and I were really great together." I smiled. "So what do you say? Do you think we should give it another try?"

He gulped, and a weird expression came over his face, sort of like a fish gasping for air. Before I could figure that one out, the mechanic under the car slid out.

"Excuse me?" she said.

Right. *She*. Those overall-clad legs turned out to belong to a dark-haired girl with bad fuchsia lipstick and a pair of enormous breasts that threatened to escape from her grimy white tank at any second and pop out over the top of her overalls.

"Um, Ava, this is Charlene," Lance said weakly. "My, uh, new girlfriend."

"Not *that* new." Charlene stood up and crossed her arms over her enormous knockers. "We've been going out for two months."

She stared at me, as if challenging me to disagree. Which, of course, I did.

"What are you talking about?" I said, wondering if those boobs had sucked all the math skills out of her brain. "Lance and I broke up less than two weeks ago."

"Right." She smirked. "And like I said, Lance and *I* hooked up two *months* ago."

As what she was saying sank in, I looked over at Lance. He was staring at his feet, looking as if he wished he were anywhere else. That told me all I needed to know. I could feel my cheeks burning.

There wasn't much left to say. I wasn't

the type to start a rumble in the parking lot of a garage, though Charlene looked as if she'd be up for it.

"Okay," I said weakly, so humiliated I couldn't even work up any real anger at the rotten, cheating two-timer in front of me. "I guess this was a big mistake. Good-bye, Lance."

I turned and walked away with as much dignity as I could muster, which wasn't much. Without looking back at them, I crawled back into the car—the front seat this time. Why not give Jason a clear shot at me? With his windows open and the nearly silent idling of that Prius engine, he had to have heard the entire thing. And this time I probably deserved all his teasing and more. Besides, he couldn't possibly make me feel any worse than I already felt. Still, I didn't dare meet his eye as I pulled the door shut and put on my seat belt.

He didn't say anything for a few minutes as he drove out of the parking lot. I figured he was gathering his thoughts for the onslaught.

Finally he cleared his throat. I braced myself.

"I've been meaning to ask you," he said

conversationally. "Have you ever been to that little Middle Eastern place in Wynnewood? Because that's where I was planning to go with Teresa tonight, only I've never tried it."

I shot him a cautious look. "Um . . . no. I've never been there. But my dad went once and said it was good."

"Cool. Your dad seems like a dude with good taste." Jason smiled. "Hummus and kebabs it is, then."

I didn't get it. Was this some meta way of teasing me by not teasing me? Before I could figure it out, my phone rang. I groaned when I saw the number. I was *so* not in the mood to deal with Camille at the moment.

But I punched the button anyway, figuring my day had nowhere to go but even farther down. "Hello?" I said wearily.

"Ava! Listen, the idiot caterers forgot to include the cake forks when they sent the tablewear over to the hall, and I have like *no* time to drive over there and pick them up, and I can't reach the wedding planner, and they're saying there's not enough time to get a delivery guy to . . . ," she babbled, barely pausing for breath.

She was so loud that her voice echoed through the car. "Camille crisis, huh?" Jason held out his hand. "Give me the phone; I'll deal with it."

Wordlessly, I handed it over. He put the phone to his face with one hand while steering the car with the other.

"Camille? This is Jason," he said. "Did you say forks? Are they at that catering warehouse in West Chester where I drove Ava and Teresa a few weeks ago?" He listened for a moment and nodded. "Okay, don't freak out. I'll go get them as soon as I drop Ava off at home."

Fifteen

I'd thought I'd been desperate before. But I hadn't even known what true desperation was until I hit on my latest plan sometime in the wee hours that night.

I'd spent several hours before that tossing and turning, trying to convince myself that I really would be okay going alone as Teresa kept suggesting. But I just couldn't stop imagining the other bridesmaids whispering to one another and shooting me pitying looks. Or how I would react to Lance walking in with that girl Charlene, knowing he'd cheated on me with her. Or even how it would feel when the bride and groom had their first dance, and then everyone was invited out onto the floor, and I was stuck watching from the sidelines with my widowed great-aunt Millie and a bunch of little kids.

Desperate? More like crazy. I paused on the rose-draped doorstep of the Sanchez house on Friday morning, wondering if I really wanted to do this. Then I pictured Charlene's smirk and squared my shoulders. I *had* to do this. It was the only way.

Teresa looked surprised when she answered the door with her cell phone in one hand and a map in the other. "Ava!" she said. "What are you doing here?"

I hadn't called to tell her about the ugly scene with Lance, not wanting to bum her out right before her big romantic dinner with Jason. Besides, I'd figured Jason would fill her in. He might have been able to resist kicking me when I was down yesterday, but I was sure he wouldn't be able to resist telling that kind of juicy story, especially at my expense.

"Hi," I said, stepping into the spacious foyer. Teresa's suitcases were stacked just inside the door, and a mess of tickets, money, and her passport was on the narrow divan by the stairs. "Good, I guess Jason's not here yet."

"Jason? Why would he be here?" She was looking more confused by the second.

"Oh." I blinked, surprised. "I just assumed he was driving you to the airport."

"No. My dad's taking me." Teresa checked her watch. "We're leaving in, like, ten minutes. Why? What's going on? Is something wrong?"

She seemed distracted, and no wonder. Here I was, barging in on her just moments before she left for a month in another country. I knew that was stretching the bounds of best-friend-dom, and I was about to stretch it even further.

"This will only take a second," I said, plunging on before I lost my nerve. "I just need to talk to you about something. Actually, I need to ask you the hugest favor in the world."

"Okay." She leaned over and flipped open one of the suitcases, sticking the map inside. "What is it?"

I could tell she still wasn't paying full attention to me. But that changed with my next words: "Can I borrow Jason to take to the wedding?"

She stood up so fast I was surprised she didn't tip over backward. "What?"

It takes a lot to shock Teresa. But I could tell she was shocked now.

"Please, just hear me out," I said quickly, not wanting to let her say no without thinking about it—though of course I wouldn't have blamed her. It was a pretty crazy request. "Obviously, we would totally be going as totally platonic friends. Totally. But that way I don't have to walk in alone, and he would look good in the photos and stuff. And he'd get a nice free meal out of it—much better than tacos at Moe's." I took a quick breath, not quite daring to meet her eye just yet. "And since it won't be a romantic thing for either of us, I'll be free to flirt with Andy or Kwan or whoever . . ."

Finally running out of words, I glanced at her nervously. Her expression was weird—sort of blank. Then she shrugged.

"Sure," she said briskly. "I don't mind at all if you two go together. But I can't speak for him. You'll need to ask him yourself."

"Of course!" I was so relieved I was afraid I'd collapse on her pile of suitcases. "I totally wasn't expecting you to call him for me when you're about to—"

"Ready to go, Teresa?" Her father strode into the foyer at that moment. Mr. Sanchez was a former Air Force guy, and I knew he liked to keep things running on schedule. "Oh, hello, Ava," he added when he saw me. "Come to say good-bye, eh?"

I smiled at him. "Something like that."

"I'm ready, Dad." Teresa hurried over and grabbed a couple of bags from the pile.

I went to help. "Thanks, Teresa," I murmured, shooting her a grateful look as I picked up a suitcase. "I really appreciate this."

She didn't meet my look. "Uh-huh," she said. "Not a big deal."

I bit my lip. She sounded kind of weird. Was she just distracted and thinking about her trip? Or was there more to it?

"Okay," I said, feeling helpless. I couldn't exactly grab her and force her to talk more about this. Not now, with her father standing right there jingling his car keys and grabbing suitcases.

We hugged before she climbed into the car. "Have fun at the wedding," she said. "You'll have to e-mail me all about it afterward."

"Will do. Have a great trip." After one last squeeze I let her go.

I waved as they drove off. I couldn't quite shake the feeling that something had been left unsaid between us. But I figured it was only the weirdness of the situation combined with the bad timing. Whatever it was, we would work it out when she got back.

In any case, the one thing I knew for sure was that when Teresa said something, she meant it. And she had definitely said I could take Jason to the wedding.

Actually, that wasn't quite what she'd said. She had said that *she* didn't mind if we went together. So now I had to convince *him*.

Now that I thought about it, I wondered if that was the explanation for Teresa's odd reaction. Maybe Jason had told her something she hadn't shared with me—like, that he couldn't stand the sight of me and only tolerated my company for her sake. Actually, that wouldn't be too surprising, considering that that was basically my reaction toward *him*.

But I wasn't going to let a little thing like mutual dislike stop me. Not now, when I was so close to finally landing a decent-looking and reliable guy who *definitely* didn't already have a date to this wedding.

I checked the time. It was a few minutes after nine, so I figured Jason would probably be up by now.

His house phone rang and rang, then went to the answering machine. I hung up without leaving a message and tried his cell. That rang once and then went to voice mail.

I hung up again without leaving a message. Maybe he was on the other line with Teresa right now. For a second I even dared to hope that she might do the hard part for me by telling him my plan.

Realizing that my stomach was growling—I'd rushed out of the house without breakfast—I decided to walk over to Lancaster Avenue and grab a muffin or something. After a couple of blocks I tried calling Jason's cell again, with the same result.

"Come on!" I muttered, punching the button to end the call a little more violently than necessary. Now that I was this close, I just wanted to seal the deal so I could relax.

Well, maybe "relax" was too strong a word. I knew that the hours between now and the rehearsal dinner that evening would probably be filled with nonstop Camille-fueled craziness as the countdown to tomorrow kicked into overdrive. It would be nice to get this out of the way before that started.

I waited until after I'd reached the

avenue and bought myself a cup of coffee and a blueberry muffin before trying again. Sitting down on the cement wall separating one parking lot from the next, I set my food beside me and then hit redial. Again the phone rang once and bounced to voice mail.

"Oh my God, where *is* he?" I cried as I hung up, attracting curious stares from a trio of preteen boys skateboarding nearby.

Teresa wasn't much of a phone talker. I doubted she would be chatting with Jason for more than twenty minutes even on the verge of a monthlong separation. So maybe he wasn't on the phone at all; maybe he'd turned it off.

I gulped down my coffee and muffin as I tried to decide what to do now. It was kind of ironic, really—for the past six months it had seemed I couldn't turn around without finding Jason there smirking at me. I couldn't get rid of the guy. And now that I actually *wanted* to see him for a change? Poof! He had disappeared.

His house was miles away, too far to walk. I considered hopping on the train or bus over there to see if he was still asleep, but I decided against it. With my luck, by the time I got there he would be gone.

Instead I figured I could check a few of his favorite local haunts. What else could I do?

He obviously hadn't been in the coffee shop, so I walked down the block to a popular diner where I knew he went sometimes. The place was packed with people chowing down on scrambled eggs and bacon, but there was no sign of Jason.

I glanced across the street at Burrito Moe's. Until this moment I hadn't even realized it was open for breakfast—who eats tacos at that hour?—but there were a few cars in the parking lot. None of those cars was a blue Prius, but I still walked across and took a look inside. No Jason.

Finally I gave up, realizing I was just wasting time. I dialed his cell number again, and this time when the voice mail came on, I left a message.

"Hi, Jason," I said. "It's Ava. Listen, you know about my wedding-date issues, right? Well, I just had a thought. How would you like to be my date? Just friends and all that, of course—oh, and I checked with Teresa before she left, and she's cool with it. So— what do you say? Feel like dressing up in a suit tomorrow, eating some fancy olives, and watching my relatives get drunk and do the chicken dance? Oh, and the rehearsal dinner is tonight, if you're up for that too. Call me."

I hung up, belatedly wondering if this whole plan had been an idiotic idea in the first place. Oh, well. It was too late now. All I could do was wait for him to get back to me.

I didn't have long to wait. My phone rang when I was only halfway home. It was Jason.

"Hey," he said. "It's me."

"Hi." There was a lot of background noise on his end, and I had a little trouble hearing him. "Where are you?"

"Sea Isle City."

My heart sank. "You mean you're at the beach? I had no idea you were going down there this weekend." So much for that plan!

"I wasn't," he replied. "I mean, I just came for the day. Sort of an impulse thing."

"Oh." My heart sort of paused on its downward plummet. "So, um, I guess you got my message? . . . "

"Uh-huh. I don't think I'll be back in time for the rehearsal dinner. But the wedding's a go."

"Really?" I sucked in my breath, hardly

daring to believe there wasn't a punchline coming. "So you'll go with me?"

"Sure, what the heck."

"Oh, that's great! I was afraid at this point I'd be stuck going by myself since every guy on the East Coast already had a date, and then last night I realized, hey, I know one guy who doesn't, and—"

"Yeah," he interrupted. "Plus this way I actually get to see you with that pink dress all the way on instead of half over your head. Good times." He chuckled. "Look, I've got to go. I'll see you tomorrow."

He hung up before I could answer. I stared at the phone, still a bit stunned. What had I just gotten myself into?

I felt anxious all the rest of that day and evening. It was a little awkward being at the rehearsal dinner dateless, having to explain my situation over and over again. The conversation usually went something like this:

Concerned-looking bridesmaid/relative/obscure-friend-of-Camille's: Oh, Ava. Here on your own, huh?

Me: Yep, my wedding date couldn't make it tonight.

CLB/R/O-F-O-C's (now with surprised look): Oh, so you *do* have a date, then?

Me (trying to head off any possible mis-understandings up front): Yes, I'm going with my friend Teresa's boyfriend, Jason.

CLB/R/O-F-O-C's: Oh! Your best friend's boyfriend? That's . . . very modern of you.

Me (trying not to sound defensive and/or pathetic): It's no big deal. I just thought we'd have fun.

CLB/R/O-F-O-C's: Wait, but I thought you were taking some super awesome mys-tery man?

Me (with forced chuckle): Oh, I was just kidding around about that. . . .

A few of the questioners also made dorky little jokes about me going with Jason, while others looked politely skepti-cal of the whole story. By the end of the evening I was wondering if it might have been easier just to hire a paid escort for the weekend. Why hadn't I thought of that earlier? In any case I figured if people were that fascinated by the sister of the bride showing up alone to the rehearsal dinner, it was nothing compared to the embarrass-ment I would have suffered if I'd had to show up to the actual wedding all alone.

Even going with Jason was definitely better than that. Wasn't it?

Sixteen

"Wow," I said when I opened the door the next day to see Jason standing there. "You look great!"

"Thanks." He did a little twirl on the front porch like a fashion model. "So do you. That dress isn't anywhere near as bad as you keep saying it is."

I wasn't sure how much of a compliment that really was, but I smiled, glancing down briefly at the Pink Horror before averting my eyes from it once again. "Thanks."

"You're welcome." He grinned at me and straightened his tie.

I couldn't believe the big day had arrived without some disaster befalling him: his car breaking down on the way home from the beach, a sudden onset of food poisoning from a bad oyster, getting struck by a meteor . . . With the way things had been going lately, I wouldn't have been too surprised by any of them.

But here he was, looking rather disarmingly handsome in his dark suit and tie. "So am I supposed to wait out here on the porch until it's time to leave, or what?" he said after a moment of me standing there staring at him.

"Oh! Sorry." I blushed and stepped back. "Come on in. Things are a little crazy around here today."

That was an understatement. We were all supposed to be over at the site for photos in less than an hour, and the kitchen table was littered with last-minute paperwork, the gifts weren't packed up yet, and Camille's hair was still in curlers. Fortunately, whatever weird mood Jason had been in the other day appeared to have passed, and he threw himself into helping with whatever needed doing. His constant jokes and goofy comments even helped distract Camille a little whenever she seemed on the verge of hyperventilating.

There were a few moments of weirdness, like when my grandparents came in while everyone except Camille was in the kitchen. "Hello, people!" my grandpa boomed, rushing over to give my mother a hug and my dad a big handshake. "What's the word? Ava! My gorgeous granddaughter! So, when are *you* getting married?"

I smiled and hugged him. "Don't hold your breath, Grandpa."

He guffawed, then turned to smile at Jason. "And who have we here?"

"This is my, uh, date. Jason." It felt strange to say that. But what the heck—it was true, right? I didn't bother going into detail about Teresa and all the rest. It only would have confused him.

Almost before I knew it we were all walking into the estate gardens where the photographer was waiting for us. "Oh, my God," Camille said as soon as we came within sight of the largest arbor. "Those roses are *red*! They totally clash with the dresses!"

"I told her not to do pink," I muttered under my breath.

Mom, Dad, the photographer, and several other members of the wedding party all started talking at once. Then Jason stepped forward.

"Check it out." He pointed across the gardens to a different, smaller arbor. "There's a bunch of white roses. How about doing it over there?"

The photographer looked relieved. "Perfect!" she said. "Is that all right, Camille?"

Camille frowned, then shrugged. "I suppose so," she said, smoothing out the fabric of her gown.

"Thanks," I whispered to Jason as we all headed over. "That was a totally obvious solution. But knowing my family, we never would have noticed. At least not before Camille insisted on, like, someone painting all the red roses pink or something."

He smiled. "I aim to please."

Camille wanted photos of all of us with our dates even if they weren't in the wedding party, and it felt a little bizarre to pose with Jason's arm around me just like a real boyfriend or something. For a second I had this weird sort of parallel-world feeling about it. Then as the photographer finished setting up a shot of the two of us, Jason leaned a little closer.

"Uh-oh," he whispered. "Your SpongeBobs are showing!"

Great. That was one photo that wouldn't

be making it to the wedding album. Not with me snarling like that.

"Let's try this one again," the photographer called tactfully. "Ready, guys? One, two, three . . ."

I gasped as Jason suddenly grabbed me around the waist and planted a big kiss on my cheek. "Hey!" I cried, just as I heard the camera click again. "What are you doing?"

He grinned. "Just getting into the spirit of the day."

"Well, quit it!" I wasn't sure whether I was more embarrassed about what Teresa would say when she saw that shot, or about how my heart had sort of thumped weirdly when he'd done it, almost as if he were a real guy and this were a real date.

I forgot about everything else for a while as we headed inside for the ceremony. Since Jason wasn't in the wedding party, he went and sat down with some of the other bridesmaids' dates while we did our thing. I was relieved to have him out of my hair for a while. He was turning out to be more distracting than I'd expected—sometimes in a good way, like when he was helping defuse a Camille meltdown, and sometimes in an oddly unsettling way, like with his antics during the photographs.

Despite Camille's best efforts to find something wrong, the ceremony went off without a hitch. Actually, it was really nice. During the exchange of vows, when Camille and Boring Bob stood up there hand in hand, staring at each other as if they couldn't get enough, I felt tears well up in my eyes. No matter how boring they might be, they were obviously head over heels gaga in love. I wondered if I would ever feel that strongly about anyone. In any case I was happy that my crazy sister had found the One. Even if that One happened to be Boring Bob.

Afterward, once the wedding party had processed back down the aisle, Camille found me in the hallway and gave me a hug. Her face was pink with joy and excitement. "Oh, Ava!" she exclaimed into my ear. "Wasn't it amazing? Can you believe Bob and I are *married*?" She held out her ring and stared at it, as if it hadn't quite sunk in.

"Congratulations, Camille," I said with a smile.

"Thanks." She sighed happily. "You know, I can't believe I got so worked up about all the plans and details and everything. In the end, none of that stuff really mattered, you know? The only important thing was what just happened in there."

I figured we'd see how true that was if the caterers overcooked the salmon or something. But I kept quiet and just smiled back at her. For now, at least, the sane Camille had returned.

"Anyway, I'm not sure why I let myself get so freaked out about it all," Camille continued. "The point of the whole thing isn't anything to do with the cake or the flowers or whatever. It's that I get to spend the rest of my life with the guy who makes my heart go thumpity-thump every time he kisses me." She beamed at me as if she'd just discovered the secret of life. Which, come to think of it, maybe she had. "I hope you find that guy someday too, Ava."

"Camille! Hey, where's my wife?" Bob appeared in the doorway, his face bright red and plastered with a giddy grin. "Come on, it's time for the receiving line."

"Coming, hubby dear!" Camille giggled, then gathered up her skirts and took off.

Camille and Bob, the wedding party, and the various parents and siblings and such all lined up in the hallway between the ceremony room and the reception hall. A moment later the guests were released into the hallway. Jason almost immediately found me in the receiving line and inserted himself in beside me. "That was nice, wasn't it?" he said. "I was glad to see you didn't trip and flash your SpongeBobs at the audience, either."

"I did my best. By the way, did anyone ever tell you it's not normal to be obsessed with other people's underwear?" I smiled and shook the hand of some friends of my parents who were making their way down the line. Jason reached out and did the same, jovially thanking them for coming.

"I'm not obsessed with other people's underwear," he said when they'd moved on. "Only yours. Hello!" he added as Mr. Baum and his wife reached us. "Thanks for being here! Wasn't it a wonderful ceremony?"

I shot him a look when the Baums had moved on as well. "Technically, you're not supposed to be part of the receiving line," I reminded him.

He grinned. "But I'm so good at it!" He smiled at the next guest in line. "Thanks for coming. Great to see you!"

I rolled my eyes. What was the point in arguing?

My stomach grumbled a little, and I realized I'd barely eaten anything all day. I glanced down the line to see how many more people were left before we could go eat, and my heart stopped. Lance was making his way down the line—with Charlene clinging to his arm! Her hair was piled on top of her head, her makeup appeared to have been troweled on, and her low-cut red dress did nothing to disguise her most noticeable assets.

Jason must have heard me gasp, because he looked over. "Hey," he said. "Isn't that the jerk who dumped you? What's he doing here?"

"He's related to the groom," I said through lips that seemed to have gone numb. I should have known that Lance wouldn't have the class to stay away today. But I'd never *really* imagined he would actually bring *her*.

Before I could fully recover from the unpleasant surprise, they were upon us. "Um, nice wedding," Lance mumbled, looking vaguely sheepish. He stuck out his hand, and I noticed his fingernails were filthy.

I gritted my teeth, forcing myself to shake his hand instead of doing what I *really* wanted to do, which was to punch him in the face. He wasn't worth ruining Camille's big day over, I told myself.

Charlene smirked at me and held out her hand like a limp fish. "Nice dress," she said. "Don't take this the wrong way, but pink isn't really your color, sweetie."

I glared at her, too furious to speak. Lance stared at the floor and shuffled his feet. The bridesmaid standing to my right glanced over in surprise, as if not sure she'd heard what she thought she'd heard.

To my left, Jason stuck out his hand to Lance. "It's, like, Lars or something, right, dude?" he said in a jovial tone. "Glad you could make it. It's always good to see a couple that really *deserves* each other, isn't it?" He shot a meaningful look at Charlene.

Lance blinked, looking confused. "Um, yeah."

Jason slung an arm around my shoulders, then turned his pleasant smile on Charlene. "And if you see anyone giving you funny looks, don't worry—it's probably just because they're wondering if you might steal their dates or something. It's definitely not anything to do with that, er, interesting fashion choice of yours. Sweetie."

Charlene scowled, looking outraged. "Hey!" she began.

But Lance yanked her past us before she could get started. "Come on," he muttered. "This wedding is a drag. Let's get out of here."

Jason smiled and waved as they hurried on. "Enjoy the reception, you two!" he called out cheerily.

I shot him a grateful glance, but he wasn't looking at me, having turned his attention to the next person in line. As I did the same, I couldn't help feeling a rush of warm fuzzies toward my "date." Going with him had started off as making the best of a bad situation, but now I was actually glad he was there. I would really owe Teresa for the loan once she got back.

Seventeen

The reception was big, lavish, and crowded. The band was playing with enthusiasm, the bartenders were doing a brisk business, and half a dozen servers were circulating with trays of canapés. I wished I could change out of the Pink Horror, but Camille had practically fainted when I'd mentioned that idea. Oh, well.

Aside from that, though, I was ready to relax and have fun. It had been a long year—*really* long. This party was our reward for surviving Camzilla for all that time. At least that was how I saw it.

Besides, after the past couple of weeks of crazy dating—not to mention my little chat with Camille right after the ceremony—I was feeling inspired to get my love life back on track. Maybe I could find that thumpity-thump-heart guy my sister was talking about. Maybe he was even here tonight, I thought with a shiver as I spotted Andy over near the dance floor chatting with some other old friends from school.

"Hey, I'll catch you later, okay?" I said to Jason soon after we'd walked in. "I'm going to say hi to Andy."

"I'll come with you," he said immediately.

I frowned. That wasn't the response I'd expected. "Um, that's okay," I said. "You don't have to—you know—keep pretending this is a real date or anything. Feel free to hang out with the guys and talk b-ball or whatever. I'll see you when they serve dinner."

This time I didn't give him a chance to respond. I just scooted off across the room without a backward glance. I felt a little guilty for ditching him, but I pushed the feeling aside. Jason was a big boy, he knew plenty of people at the wedding, and he wasn't shy. What was the big deal?

Andy saw me coming and smiled. "Hey, Ava," he said, raising his glass to me. "Nice dress."

"Please!" I rolled my eyes. "Can you believe Camille actually made me wear pink?"

He laughed. "Yeah, I know. I remember back in high school when they wanted you to wear that pink sash for the spring choir concert, and you—"

"Ah, there's my lovely date!" Jason appeared at my shoulder, grinning and holding two glasses. "I've been searching this whole place for you, Ava. Here you go—iced tea. Your favorite, right?"

I shot him a glare. What was he up to? I'd only left him five minutes ago—barely enough time to go grab those drinks, let alone "search" for me. What was he doing?

"Thanks," I said through clenched teeth. "Andy, you remember Jason? He was at the pool party with Teresa."

"Sure. Hey, man." Andy shook Jason's hand. "So did you say you're Ava's date today?"

"That's right." He reached over and threw an arm around my shoulders. I did my best to shake it off, but he just squeezed more tightly. "I'm a lucky guy, huh?"

"Sure." Andy looked a little confused. And no wonder—Jason was acting like a total freak. Was this his way of having fun at this wedding? Torturing me? And here I'd just been thinking how sweet he was acting. . . .

"Excuse me," I said. "I need to take a trip to the little girls' room." At least Jason couldn't follow me there.

I left them chatting together and hurried to the bathroom. It was painful looking in the mirror and seeing the Pink Horror, but I did my best to ignore that as I reapplied my lipstick and checked my hair.

While I was standing there, I saw a hideous blob of pink out of the corner of my eye—another bridesmaid had just entered. It was Lissa.

"Ava!" she gushed, her high-pitched voice even higher-pitched than usual and her cheeks flushed with excitement She rushed over and gave me a hug, almost knocking my favorite M.A.C. lipstick out of my hand. "Wasn't it a beautiful ceremony? Camille looked so gorgeous! And Bob was superhandsome."

As far as I was concerned, *Bob + Handsome = Does Not Compute.* But I kept that opinion to myself.

"Yeah, it was great," I said.

She gave me a little pinch on the arm

and a conspiratorial smile. "And that date of yours—well, let's just say I can see why you kept him under wraps. Hubba hubba!"

I was surprised. Firstly, because I didn't think anyone outside a Saturday morning cartoon actually said "hubba hubba." Secondly, because Lissa didn't seem to realize that Jason wasn't a "hubba hubba" kind of date. It didn't seem worth trying to explain that to her, though, so I just smiled and headed for the door.

"See you later," I said. I could only hope her head wouldn't explode if she happened to see me slow-dancing with Andy later that evening.

As I stepped out of the restroom, I immediately spotted Andy over near the bandstand talking to Emily, an old high-school classmate of Teresa's who had taken tennis lessons from Camille for a while. I smiled and made a beeline for him.

Halfway there, Jason appeared and stepped in front of me. "Hi!" he said brightly. "I love this song. Want to dance?"

"Maybe later," I said, dodging around him.

But he sidestepped neatly, blocking me again. "Aw, come on," he wheedled with a grin. "You shouldn't diss me until you've seen my moves." He did a goofy little hip wriggle.

I rolled my eyes. "You call that a move?"

"That's nothing," he bragged. "Check this out!"

He grabbed me by the hand and waist and spun me around so suddenly that I almost tripped over my dyed-pink pumps. Then, before I could protest, he dipped me.

"Hey!" I exclaimed once I was upright again. "Do you mind? Most polite people *ask* before they just start flinging other people around."

"I did ask, remember?" He kept dancing on his own, grooving out to the song that was playing.

"Okay, but I don't remember saying yes." Glancing around, I saw that his solo dancing was attracting attention from the people nearby. A couple of older ladies were watching and clapping along. A little farther away, Andy was looking at Jason with a confused expression.

"Would you knock it off?" I said to Jason. "People are staring."

"That always happens when I get down with my bad self," he responded, throwing in a little *Saturday Night Fever* finger-pointing move.

That particular move aside, I had to admit he wasn't a bad dancer. Still, I was relieved when the band cut off and the singer announced that it was time for Camille and Bob's first dance.

The whole crowd gathered around as Boring Bob gave a rather gallant bow before a blushing Camille. It was actually pretty cute. They danced with each other, and then my dad cut in, and Bob went and pulled his mom out of the crowd . . . the whole deal.

I shuffled back a bit, hoping to sidle closer to Andy before everyone was invited out to join in the dance. He was standing just a few yards away now, and I managed to work my way through the crowd until I was right next to him.

"Hey," I murmured. "Having fun?"

He smiled at me. "Yeah. You?"

"More and more by the minute." I smiled back, hoping he got the message.

"All right, everyone," the bandleader said into the microphone. "Let's have all the happy couples in the room get out there and . . ."

I tilted my head up toward Andy with a friendly sort of look on my face. If he didn't ask me to dance right away, I was fully prepared to do the asking myself.

But just then Jason appeared. "Hey, Ava," he said. "You're needed for some kind of errand."

"Huh?" I had a horrible flashback to the zillions of errands I'd been sent on over the past ten or twelve months—everything from picking up the invitations at the printer to shuttling Camille's dress around town to that ridiculous wild-goose chase after the olives. I'd thought I was finished with all that. "What is it?"

Jason just shrugged and shot an apologetic look at Andy. "Mind if I borrow her for a while?"

"Sure."

I sighed and followed him to the edge of the crowd around the dance floor. And here I'd thought Camille had finally returned to sanity. . . .

"Okay, so what is it?" I asked Jason when we were in the clear.

"Nothing," he replied. "Just wanted to rescue you before someone dragged you out to dance. I know how much you hate dancing." He shot me a completely infuriating little grin.

"Oh, please!" I exclaimed. "Just because I didn't want to dance with *you* doesn't mean I . . . aargh!" Realizing I was wasting my time arguing with him—and worse yet giving him exactly what he wanted—I whirled around and stomped away, heading for the French doors leading out to the garden so I could get some air.

My dad's cousin Sally reached out to me as I went by. She was half blind without her glasses, which she was too vain to wear in public, so she probably couldn't see the expression on my face. I was surprised she could even recognize me. Maybe she'd just been grabbing every blurry pink blob that went by until she got lucky.

"Ava, dear!" she trilled. "Wasn't it a lovely ceremony?"

"Great, Cousin Sally," I said, forcing myself to sound pleasant and polite. After all, it wasn't her fault my "date" was an obnoxious child. "Just fantastic."

"Totally fantastic!" Jason said, appearing at my side. "It's Cousin Sally, right? You look lovely this evening. I'm Ava's date, Jason—we met in the receiving line."

"Oh, yes!" Cousin Sally giggled. "Ava, what a charming young man you found for yourself!"

"Yeah." I shot Jason a scowl, knowing that Sally probably wouldn't be able to see it. "He's a charmer, all right."

After that I found myself waylaid by a parade of relatives and other guests. The entire time Jason hovered at my side, playing the part of an attentive date and probably chortling on the inside the whole time. I'd known he was easily amused, but I didn't quite get the joke this time. Did he really get his jollies from irritating people?

I eventually got my revenge when we encountered my uncle Phil over by the windows overlooking the gardens. "Say, Uncle Phil," I said brightly. "Jason here was just telling me how much he loves hearing stories from the good old days. Why don't you tell him that one about how you started your first business when you were still in high school?"

Phil's face lit up. "Oh, my boy!" he exclaimed, clutching at Jason's arm with one wizened hand. "Have I got a tale for you. . . ."

"Excuse me, I'll be right back," I said,

ducking away as Phil launched into one of his long, rambling stories. As soon as my back was turned, I broke out in a big grin. Not only had I just made an old man very happy, but Jason was sure to be stuck there listening for a good long time. Talk about multitasking!

Now, *finally*, maybe I could see about getting better reacquainted with Andy. He wasn't sitting at his assigned table, so I started circulating, keeping an eye out for him.

I finally spotted him out on the dance floor. A slow dance was playing, and for a second I assumed he was dancing with his platonic date, Mariella Farley. But if that was the case, why was he holding her so close? . . .

I gasped as the couple swayed and turned. That wasn't Mariella—it was Emily, the girl from school I'd seen him talking to earlier. Now that I thought about it, she was an ex of Andy's too. They'd dated for almost a year back when they were both sopho-mores.

I saw Andy run his hands up and down her back. Emily tilted her head back, smiled, and said something I couldn't hear at that distance. Andy smiled back, leaned closer . . . and they shared a long, lingering kiss!

I backed away, my heart sinking. It seemed that Andy really was going to revive an old relationship tonight. Just not with me.

I couldn't help feeling dejected and a little bit *re*jected. It was hard to avoid wondering whether things might have turned out differently if I'd had the chance to spend time with Andy earlier in the evening.

Either way, it didn't really matter. Obviously, he was back with Emily now, and that was that. I liked Emily too much to try to interfere. Besides, I wasn't the type of girl to try to steal a guy from another girl. There were too many guys in the world to stoop to that. At least that had always been my philosophy.

As I turned away from the happy couple, the crowd parted and I spotted Kwan, the hot guy from Teresa's barn. I hadn't seen him at all during the ceremony, and he must have skipped the receiving line. Now I felt a little jolt at the sight of him. If he'd been handsome in riding breeches, he was downright stunning in formalwear. He was standing alone on the other side of the dance floor watching the swaying couples.

My bummed-out mood passed instantly. Andy who? Maybe this was fate working for me again. . . .

Just then Jason appeared at my shoulder. "Wow, that uncle of yours can talk." He looked out at the dance floor and raised an eyebrow. "Hey, isn't that one of your many boyfriends out there slobbering all over that chick?"

"Is it? I hadn't noticed. Well, if you'll excuse me . . ." I hurried off in Kwan's direction.

I should have known I wouldn't get away that easily. Jason kept step beside me. "So what do you want to do now, my little datey-date?" he asked with a smirk.

I gritted my teeth. How could Teresa ever have fallen for someone so *obnoxious*?

Eighteen

Jason stuck to me like glue for the next hour and a half. Part of the time he had an excuse, since we were seated together for dinner. But there was no good reason he had to follow me to the bar in search of a lemon slice for my iced tea. Or stand there with a hand on my arm while Camille and Boring Bob cut the cake. Or insert himself into every conversation I had with a friend or relative.

Finally I had to resort to the ladies' room trick again to lose him. I excused myself, leaving Jason chatting with my aunt Hazel, and hurried off in search of Kwan.

I found him standing by himself near the bar. "Oh, hi, Kwan!" I said, feigning surprise. "Remember me, Ava? We met at the barn last week."

"Of course." He smiled and seemed genuinely glad to see me. "You looked great up there earlier." He waved vaguely at the Pink Horror to indicate my maid-of-honor role.

"Thanks. So are you having fun?"

"Sure." He shrugged. "It's a great party. I just wish I knew more people." He laughed sheepishly. "My date ditched me to go line-dance with her friends, so here I am."

I glanced over at the dance floor. Kwan's date, Ashley Weiss, was there among a giggling group of girls her age. The line dance they were doing didn't really match the song the band was playing, but they didn't seem to mind.

"Well, don't worry," I told Kwan. "I'm here to rescue you from boredom and loneliness."

He laughed. "That's nice of you," he said. "I hope your boyfriend doesn't mind."

"My boyfriend?" I shook my head quickly. "No, no. You mean the guy I'm here with? He's just a friend. Actually, he's Teresa's boyfriend."

"Really?"

I swallowed back a sigh. Why did everyone look so surprised when I told them that? Hadn't a girl ever borrowed her friend's guy before?

"See, since Teresa is away, we decided—"

"Ava!"

I couldn't believe it. It was Jason—again.

He sauntered up to us, grinning. "Hey, I thought you were going to the little girls' room," he said. "You weren't just trying to ditch me, were you?"

"Not at all," I said through clenched teeth, doing my best to sound pleasant for Kwan's sake. "I just stopped to say hi to someone on the way."

Jason turned and stuck out his hand to Kwan. "Hi," he said. "I'm Jason."

I left the two of them getting acquainted and dashed for the ladies' room—for real this time. I needed time to cool off. When was Jason going to get tired of this annoying little game?

When I emerged from the ladies' room a few minutes later, Jason was loitering around just outside. There was no sign of Kwan.

"Where'd he go?" I asked, glancing around.

"Who, you mean that dude Kwan?" Jason nodded toward the French doors a little way away. "He went outside."

"Outside?"

"Yeah. Something about having a smoke." Jason pursed his lips and took an imaginary toke. "And I don't think he's into cigarettes, if you know what I mean."

I was surprised and a little disappointed. My mind immediately flashed to Andy and his crazy cannabis habit back in high school. What was it with me being attracted to guys who liked to get high?

Still, I reminded myself, just because Kwan might have a smoke once in a while, that didn't mean he was as into it as Andy had been back then. I would just have to get to know him better and see what was what.

Just then Kwan himself appeared in the doorway. "Hey," he greeted me and Jason with a smile. "Nice gardens. Those big red roses just outside smell great."

"Really?" I said with what I hoped was a cool, playful smirk. "Great enough to cover a certain—you know—smell?" I mimed a toke, just as Jason had a moment earlier.

"Huh?" Kwan blinked at me.

"It's okay." I shrugged. "I'm not going

to, like, narc you out to my sister or anything. I know this wedding is probably kind of a drag if you don't know anyone—I don't blame you for wanting to take the edge off, you know?" I took another imaginary drag and winked at him.

He scowled. "Wait a minute," he said. "Are you accusing me of something?"

"Accusing? No!" I said quickly. He looked kind of insulted. "Like I said, it's no big deal. I mean, I'm not into that stuff myself, but I know lots of people who get stoned once in a—"

"Stoned?" he exclaimed, interrupting me. "Are you kidding? I don't touch that stuff!"

"Okay, okay," I said. "Sorry, I was just joking around."

"Who do you think I am, anyway?" he cried, his face darkening with anger. "I'm a serious athlete, you know—I don't do *anything* that might jeopardize my fitness or my focus, not to mention my horse. I mean, I want to make it to the Olympics someday!"

"I'm sorry," I said when he paused for breath. Out of the corner of my eye I saw that Jason was smirking, and I realized I'd been had. When would I ever learn? "Kwan, really, I didn't mean . . ."

But it was too late. He was already stalking off without a backward glance.

I rounded on Jason. "Gee, thanks a lot!" I cried. "Thanks to you, he'll probably never speak to me again, now that I practically accused him of sneaking out to get high!"

"Oops!" Jason said mildly. "Guess your sense of humor is a little off tonight." He shrugged and glanced after Kwan. "And obviously that poor guy doesn't have one at all."

He shoved both hands into his pants pockets, then turned and wandered off toward the bar. Feeling red-hot anger flushing my cheeks, I stomped after him.

"Hey!" I yelled, more furious with him than I'd ever been. I grabbed his arm, digging my fingers into his flesh through his jacket sleeve. "What's your problem, anyway?"

He yanked his arm away and turned to face me. "What's *my* problem? *You're* the one who's yelling." He glanced at the people around us. "How about keeping your voice down?"

"How about *not* telling me what to do, you immature jerk?" I clenched my fists at my side, not caring who was listening. "You make me crazy, you know that, Jason? I mean, every time I start thinking that maybe, just *maybe* there might be a nice guy in there behind that smirk somewhere, you go and do something like this."

"Easy . . . ," he murmured, glancing around again.

So he was embarrassed? Good!

"How can you be such a jerk?" I exclaimed. "First you make fun of me for wanting a nice date for this wedding, and now this. I always figured you were just kidding around all those times you'd tease me or whatever. But now? Well, now I'm starting to think you're just a mean person."

By now, people nearby were definitely staring, but I didn't care. Jason had embarrassed me enough times—let him get a taste of his own medicine for once!

His smirk was totally gone by now. "Look, let's take this outside," he mumbled. He grabbed my hand and yanked me toward the nearest door. I tried to drag my heels, but ended up stumbling over them instead. Stupid three-inch pumps . . .

A moment later we were out in the garden, standing on the little cobblestone walk that looped around through the roses. We were beneath the arbor that framed the French doors. Big, poufy dark-red blossoms drooped overhead, releasing their musky scent into the breezy evening air.

But I hardly noticed any of that. I was still totally focused on hating Jason.

"Fine," I said. "I guess you don't want witnesses when I tell you exactly what I think of you, huh? No wonder—if I was a huge jerkwad like you, I wouldn't want anyone to know it either."

"Look, Ava," he said. "I was just kidding around. You know me, I—"

"Yes, unfortunately, I *do* know you," I broke in, ready to let him have it. I'd been holding it in for six months, but enough was enough. "I know you're obnoxious, and self-centered, and vain, and probably care more about your stupid hair than you do about anyone, and—"

"You know what?" he interrupted. In the moonlight I could see that he was starting to look kind of annoyed.

"What?" I asked.

He just glared at me for a second. I glared right back at him.

Then he grabbed me by both shoulders— and kissed me!

Nineteen

I was so surprised that it was a moment or two before I realized that I was just standing there kissing him back. Whoa! What was up with that?

My brain finally kicked back into gear and ordered my body to push him away and slap him across the face. Somehow, though, my body didn't seem to be obeying. In fact, it was totally rebelling. My eyes were fluttering shut. My arms were creeping up around his neck. My lips remained locked on his. And what was that? Could it be my heart . . . letting out a *thumpity-thump*?

That finally startled me out of my fog. This was all wrong. I yanked myself loose of his embrace.

"Hey!" I blurted out.

Then I just stared at him for a moment, wondering what exactly had just happened. He stared back at me. His face looked kind of red in the moonlight, and his hair, formerly perfect as usual, was a bit tousled. Somehow, both of those things made him look even cuter than normal.

He was the first to speak. "I've wanted to do that for a long time," he said.

"Wha-huh?" I replied. I was definitely having trouble taking all this in. "I, uh, you—what?"

He didn't seem to notice I was babbling like an idiot. "I thought you were cute the first time we met," he said. "More than cute, actually. But I was with Teresa then, so I just ignored those feelings."

I stared at him. By the way he was looking back at me, I could tell he expected me to say something now. But my brain seemed to be stuck in neutral.

He shrugged and went on. "Anyway, I figured it wasn't meant to be, you know? But then these past couple of weeks, spending so much time with you, I realized that what I was feeling might be too important to ignore, no matter how—you know, *complicated* it might be." He reached over and took one of my hands in both of his. "I only hope you'll give me a chance . . ."

My head was spinning, and for once I was completely speechless. Staring down at my hand lying limply in his, I tried to figure out what exactly was going on here. Was this another of his weird jokes, like the thing with Kwan?

One look at his face gave me the answer: No way. There was no trace of the Smirk. Only sincerity shining out from his eyes. Could this earnest, adorable guy—who just happened to be an amazing kisser, by the way—really be the same obnoxious Jason I'd loathed for so long?

Or had I really loathed him? Sure, I'd always complained about all his teasing, his little jokes and stupid nicknames. But at the same time, was it possible that I'd enjoyed the attention, even just a teensy little bit? Was I really that junior high?

"Um . . ." I had no idea what to say. I didn't even have any idea how to *feel*. All this time I'd been dismissing Jason as just another Boring Bob type. But now that I thought about it—*really* thought about it—I wasn't sure that was fair. Maybe Jason didn't have an overwhelming single passion like Lance and his cars, Rocco and his sports, Oliver and his music—whatever. But unlike Bob, who got the sweats if he had to go anywhere more exotic than the mailbox, Jason did seem willing to go out and do things. Lots of things, actually. Like going to see Oliver's band, or that comedy troupe. Going to the beach on impulse all by himself. A last-minute trip through the city on a search for olives and cheesesteaks. Or even taking me to this wedding with pretty much no notice.

I blinked, suddenly realizing that all that made Jason kind of an adventurous, open-minded, impulsive person. Sort of like . . . me.

I realized he was watching me carefully. "What are you thinking?" he asked.

"Just that we have a lot in common," I managed to choke out. "Or more than I thought we did, anyway."

He smiled. Squeezing my hand more tightly, he pulled me toward him. Before I quite knew what was happening, we were kissing again.

This time I didn't bother to fight it. Melting into his embrace, I closed my eyes and just let myself enjoy it. Maybe it was the moonlight, the scent of the roses surrounding us, or the aftereffects of the romantic wedding ceremony, but the moment felt so right that I couldn't help wondering if this was where fate had been leading me all along. All this time I'd been searching for something, for some*one* . . . but maybe the one I was looking for had been right under my nose the whole time. After all, hadn't we ended up here together on this big day, thanks mostly to luck, along with the generosity of . . .

Teresa! Suddenly my happy mood came crashing down around me. I shoved Jason away and jumped back, horrified by what I was doing.

"Wait, we can't do this!" I cried.

"Huh?"

"No," I mumbled, wiping my mouth as if hoping to erase the feel of his lips on mine. "This is all so, so wrong . . ." How could I betray my best friend for a guy—*any* guy? How was I ever going to make this up to her?

He was still staring at me, looking confused. "Ava?" he murmured, reaching for my hand.

I yanked it away before he could grab it. "No," I said again, near tears as the significance of what I'd just done really hit me. "We can't—I can't do this to Teresa."

Saying her name out loud put me over the edge. I dissolved into tears as I whirled away and raced off, hardly hearing him calling out my name.

It just wasn't fair. None of it. Suddenly the happiest day of my sister's life had become the most miserable and pathetic day of my own.

Twenty

"Hey, Ava! Where's the fire?"

Boring Bob's boringly jovial voice broke into my misery. I had stumbled, half blinded by tears, into the building and down some random hall. Somehow, I'd ended up in the little room set aside for the bride and groom to get away for a moment and catch their breath. Seeing that Bob and Camille were sitting very close together on the tasteful beige sofa, I suspected I'd interrupted something, but I wasn't about to worry about that. They had a whole lifetime ahead of them to grope each other.

Besides, at that particular moment my mind was such a complete whirlwind that I didn't have any room to spare for guilt about the interruption. All of my guilt and anxiety was occupied with one question: How was I going to break this to Teresa?

A few other emotions were tumbling around in there too. For instance, anger— how could Jason do this to me, not to mention Teresa, who had barely left town five seconds ago? There was also some misery— how unfair was it that the perfect guy for me happened to hook up with my best friend first? And finally, a touch of lust— would it really be *so* wrong to make out with him again?

I knew the answer to that last one. Yes. It *would* be wrong. No matter how right it had felt to kiss him, it could never happen again.

Camille got up, smoothed out the rumpled skirt of her dress, and peered at me. "Hey, what's wrong with you? You look weird."

I tried to smile, to say something casual and walk out with my dignity intact. But it was no use. I couldn't hide what I was feeling. Not this time.

"I just did something really, really stupid," I blurted out. "I just—I just kissed Jason."

Camille looked confused. "Jason? You mean as in your date Jason?"

Normally a stupid question like that would have earned a snarky response from me—something along the lines of *No, Jason Alexander. Duh.* But at the moment I didn't have the energy.

"Yeah," I said, sinking onto the edge of a handy chair. "He was really being annoying, so I was yelling at him, and we went outside, and then *poof!* We were kissing." I sighed. "I don't know what I was thinking. I *wasn't* thinking. Teresa is never going to forgive me, and I don't blame her!"

Camille and Bob traded a slightly confused glance. "Um, well, maybe she'll understand," Camille said.

"Right," Bob added. "You were just caught up in the moment, that's all. No big deal. Teresa seems like a reasonable person—she'll be okay once you explain."

"Yeah." Camille smiled at him. "Bob's right. Teresa is really down to earth. Besides, you guys have been friends forever. She won't let this come between you."

I could tell they were trying to help. They were so giddy in their own happiness right now that to them it probably seemed that no problem was insurmountable. But everything they said was only making me feel worse.

"Thanks, guys." I stood up and took a deep breath, trying to compose myself long enough to make my escape. Then maybe I could go find a nice, private corner to cry in for a while. "I guess I'll leave you to—"

"Ava!" It was Jason. He stood in the doorway, looking upset. "We need to talk."

"There's nothing to talk about," I said, not meeting his eye. "Nothing either of us can say will make this horrible nightmare go away—not unless you've figured out how to turn back time so it never happened. And if you could do that, you know, you'd probably be, like, off accepting the Nobel Prize or something and not here at some wedding cheating on your girlfriend with her best—"

"Shut up!" he yelled, interrupting my rambling monologue. He grimaced as I stared at him in surprise. "Sorry, I didn't mean to yell. But man, can you get rolling sometimes!"

Behind me I heard Camille giggle. Then she cleared her throat and went silent again.

Jason was staring at me intensely. "I

didn't cheat on anybody," he said. "Teresa and I broke up the night before she left."

"What?" I was barely aware of Camille and Bob tiptoeing past us out of the room. I was totally focused on Jason, trying to figure out the punch line here. "What do you mean, you broke up? No, you didn't—she would have told me."

"She didn't tell you?" He shrugged. "Well, it's true. In fact, when it happened, both of us admitted that we should've done it months ago. We were never really anything more than friends with benefits anyway."

"Really?" In a way what he was saying made sense. It would certainly explain that weird vibe I'd gotten from Teresa the morning she left.

But I couldn't help feeling wary. Could I really trust Jason on something like this?

"Really," he said. "The spark just wasn't there between me and Teresa. Not like, um . . ."

His voice trailed off as he reached out and took my hand. I shivered as I felt it— the spark.

I bit my lip, gazing into his eyes and seeing the same spark reflected there.

Maybe *that* was what I needed to trust— that feeling. The spark. The thumpity-thump.

I just hoped I wasn't making a huge mistake.

Camille and Bob had left the door ajar, and through it came the faint sound of the vocalist announcing the final song. The Wedding of the Century was almost over.

A second later I heard the band striking up the opening bars. It was "Last Dance," the old Donna Summer tune. Leave it to cheesy Camille to choose that as the final song at her wedding!

Jason cleared his throat. "So," he said, sounding uncharacteristically uncertain, "should we—that is, do you want to dance? You know—with me?"

I hesitated. This still felt strange. What would Teresa say if she could see us right now? Would it hurt her the way seeing Lance and his new girlfriend together had hurt me?

No way, I thought. *Teresa isn't me. Jason isn't Lance. And I'm certainly no Charlene!*

The last thought made me smile a little. Jason was watching my face carefully.

"Well?" he asked. "Don't leave me hanging, Ava."

I squeezed his hand. I wished I could talk to Teresa about this right now. It felt totally weird, and I knew it would keep feeling that way until we spoke. But in the meantime it was the middle of the night in Germany, and I could almost hear her voice in my head laughing and telling me to go for it.

"Yes," I said. "As a matter of fact, I'd love to dance."

It felt weirdly right as he took me in his arms out on the dance floor. By the time we got out there the slow part of the song was almost over. But even when the band swung into the up-tempo disco part, Jason and I kept right on slow-dancing in the middle of the floor. I was still a little nervous about what Teresa would say. But I tried to put it out of my mind for now.

Jason hugged me a little closer, bending down to sing into my ear along with the song. "Last dance," he sang softly. "SquarePants. Last dance . . ."

I laughed, wondering why I'd ever found his jokes so irritating. I wasn't sure.

But I was pretty sure about one thing. This wouldn't be our last dance together—not by a long shot.

I was still smiling when he stopped singing and kissed me, right there on the dance floor in front of everybody I knew.

"I still can't believe you didn't tell me." I speared a piece of banana pancake with my fork.

"I know," Teresa said. "Everything just seemed so rushed, you know? I wasn't thinking it would happen right then— he kind of sprang it on me that Thursday night, and it was too late to call you when I got home, and then in the morning I was so rushed . . . I mean, we'd both been kind of leaning that way for a while, but I was just assuming we'd deal with it when I got back." She took a sip of her coffee and smiled across the table at me, looking ridiculously tanned and relaxed for someone who'd been on a transatlantic flight less than twelve hours earlier. "But I guess he was in more of a hurry. For obvious reasons."

I blushed and smiled down at my plate. Even though my one-month anniversary with Jason was coming up soon, our relationship still felt new. That was a weird feeling for me. Usually by the time I'd been with a guy for a whole month, I was starting to get restless. But not this time.

"So you're really okay with this?" I asked for about the fifth time in five minutes. Of course I'd e-mailed Teresa as soon as I was home from the wedding to let her know what had happened. And we'd talked a couple of times on the phone, though the time difference and the international charges had kept those conversations short. But this was our first chance to hash it out face-to-face. We were in a quiet booth at a local diner having breakfast.

"Of course," she answered. "I mean, sure, it's a little weird. But what's life without weirdness? Especially life around you two?"

I grinned. "Oh, come on. Sure, Jason's a little weird. But me?"

"You two are a perfect match." She chuckled. "Much better than he and I were, that's for sure."

"But that's the part I don't get." I reached for the syrup. "You two always got along so well. I don't think I ever saw you fight."

She shrugged. "We were friends," she said. "We really get along that way. That's probably why neither of us worked up the energy to break up for so long. But I knew for a long time that he was never going to be the guy to make my ears tingle, you know what I mean?"

"Sure," I replied. "He wasn't your thumpity-thump guy." At her confused look, I explained, "That's Camille's term for it."

"Oh. Well, anyway, it turns out he was feeling the same way all along. So when he realized he'd found someone else who *did* make him feel that way . . ." She gave me a meaningful look.

"I still feel kind of guilty about that," I admitted, stirring my food around with my fork. "Like I, you know, stole him from you or something."

"Don't be ridiculous," she said briskly. "This is me you're talking to, remember? Besides, it's like I said. You two are so perfect together it's disgusting."

I grinned. But her comment reminded me of something that had been bugging me. "You know, a lot of people have been saying that," I said. "But I don't get it. How did I miss it for so long? Most of the time you two were dating, I just thought he was Mr. Annoying."

"Maybe that was because he was off-limits," Teresa suggested, leaning her elbows on the table. "Your subconscious translated your attraction to him into disgust."

"Who let you take that psych class last semester?" I joked. But I was still a bit perplexed. How had I missed the obvious for so long? Wasn't I the one who was always sizing up every guy I met and picturing myself with him?

Well, maybe not so much anymore . . . Jason and I had seen each other almost every day for the past month, starting with the blissfully quiet and peaceful two weeks when Camille and Bob had been away on their honeymoon. I hardly even noticed other guys anymore, and when Zoom had called once he got out of the hospital to see if I wanted to get together, I'd let him down easy—and with no regrets or second thoughts. I was like a whole new Ava. A one-guy Ava. It was kind of a nice feeling.

"So what do you two have planned for your one-month anniversary?" Teresa asked, leaning back in the squeaky vinyl booth.

"He won't tell me," I said. "Says it's a surprise."

Just then Teresa's phone buzzed. She dug it out of her purse, and her face lit up when she saw the number. "Oh, it's Helmut!" she said, sounding almost giddy. "Do you mind?"

"Go for it." I smiled as she jumped out of the booth and hurried across to a private spot near the restrooms. We'd been so busy talking about my love life that I'd only heard a little about hers so far. But her eyes had danced and her voice had gone all soft when she'd told me about Helmut, a cute German guy she'd met during her internship. It was nice to see her that way for a change. I tended to go all goofy with *any* new guy—from Lance to Zoom to Oliver to Kwan to whoever. But Teresa wasn't that way. If Helmut was making her light up like that, he had to be pretty special.

"Hey, there you are. Are you trying to hide from me back here?"

It was Jason. I felt myself light up too as he slid into the booth beside me. "Nope," I said, giving him a kiss. "Just aiming for some privacy."

He glanced around, looking adorably anxious. His hair looked perfect as always, and he was wearing a green T-shirt I'd given him that brought out the color of his eyes.

"Where's, uh, you know, Teresa?" he asked.

"Over there." I nodded toward the corner where she was huddled over the phone with her back to us, totally oblivious to his arrival. "She'll be back in a minute."

"I really hope she's okay with this," he said, sounding nervous. "You know—us."

"She is," I assured him. Then I reached over and wrapped my arms around him. "She totally is."

He smiled and leaned forward to kiss me. My heart went thumpity-thump, my ears tingled, and I felt that spark flare up as strongly as ever. What had I ever seen in all those other guys, anyway? It was as if they'd never really existed. Jason was the only guy in the world for me now. No joke.

About the Author

Catherine Hapka has some experience with pink bridesmaid dresses . . . but luckily, she looks just fine in pink. She has written more than one hundred and fifty books for children and young adults. In addition to reading and writing, she enjoys horseback riding, animals of all kinds, gardening, music, and traveling. She lives on a small farm in Chester County, Pennsylvania, with a horse, three goats, a small flock of chickens, and too many cats.

The energy in the reception hall felt charged. Dance floor in full bloom, the buzz of conversation hummed against lively music. Waiters in black ties darted throughout the ballroom, balancing trays spiked with bubbling champagne flutes. Sara Sullivan hardly noticed the giddy group of bridesmaids that had gathered in a corner near the stage.

It was only about the millionth time in her fifteen-year-old life that she'd attended a party where she was neither guest nor hostess. Her exact title was "assistant to the event planner"—the event planner being her mother. At this particular party it had been hard to focus on assisting with anything. She'd practically abandoned her responsibilities as she became fully enraptured with the cutest guy she'd ever seen in her life.

From the back of the reception hall she gazed at dark curls, sun-kissed skin, a perfectly chiseled jaw, and sculpted broad shoulders. He had the rare combination of dark hair and blue eyes, and she swore his eyelashes cast a shadow over his cheeks. He was new in the band and he stood out like a palm tree in Alaska. Much younger than the rest of his bandmates, he looked like he didn't belong in the band-issued suit he wore. The only thing that seemed to fit him was the guitar he held.

A crackle came from her headset. She waited to hear her mother's voice, but there was nothing.

"Mom?"

No reply.

Odd, she thought. She wondered if Cute New Guitar Guy liked girls who wore headsets. She felt so dorky sometimes.

When she glanced back at the stage, he was watching her. She didn't give her eyes a chance to introduce themselves to his, and quickly looked at the clipboard she held. Why was she so shy and weird when it came to cute boys? Now she looked antisocial with a headset. A confident smile with lingering eye contact would've been nice. No, instead she had to be the nervous-looking chick with wire pinching the sides of her caramel-colored bangs.

"I can't find your mother anywhere." The agitated voice took Sara by surprise. Sara turned to face the mother of the bride. One look at her and Sara knew the woman had come with trouble. A vein spidered down the side of her temple, slithering beneath the high collar of her taupe sequined gown, and her pointy eyebrows were all scrunched up.

"I am not watching a ten-thousand-dollar cake end up all over the soles of that man's Air Jordans." She threw a thumb over her shoulder. "I don't care who he is."

A crowd had gathered near the cake. In spite of Sara's five-two frame, she could still make out the tip of the bride's veil somewhere inside the fray. She had no idea what was going on, but she headed toward the crowd, the mother of the bride marching closely behind her.

"Mom, you there?" Sara spoke into the microphone on her headset. "Potential RM. I repeat, potential RM." They had all kinds of codes, but RM was code for disaster. It actually stood for Regina Manfrankler. Sara and her mother had made up the code last year after the ambitious Regina Manfrankler had shown up at the wedding of her ex-boyfriend equipped with three cans of red spray paint she'd reserved for the entire wedding party.

Sara and Leah found her tagging the white bridal limo with THE GROOM HAS A SMALL . . . They stopped her before she divulged the details, then covered her words with streamers and whipped cream. Sara had been pretty certain that what Regina had planned to say didn't involve the groom's bank account.

Sara made her way to the group, and as far as she could tell, everyone looked happy. A smile covered the bride's face as she shimmied with the music. The yellow bridesmaids' dresses swished with each step. So what could the problem be? It wasn't until Sara was up close that she noticed the potential RM. On his back, legs spinning around the floor like the top of a Black Hawk was the tallest man Sara had ever seen in her fifteen years on earth. His name was Mickey Piper. In the world of basketball he was famous. He was also the best man at this wedding.

Sara didn't care if he had ten pairs of sneakers and a video game in his name. All she cared about was that he was break-dancing within a millimeter of the wedding cake. This wasn't any old cake. This was a delicacy adorned with rare edible flowers that had been delivered from the south of France—a pastry chef's masterpiece that boasted real diamonds atop the bride and groom figurines. Sara and her mother had spent more time making sure this cake turned out okay than most girls spend picking out homecoming gowns. He must be stopped at once.

But how? This was not her kind of crisis. Her list of responsibilities included bustling the bride's dress and making sure each guest left with a wedding favor. This was clearly a crisis reserved for someone with more experience. She tried her mother again. Still nothing. She watched Mickey Piper for a moment. She knew it was twisted but she couldn't help but wonder if the videographer was catching all this. How often did famous basketball players breakdance at weddings?

She'd witnessed her fair share of wedding idiots. When your mother is an event planner, brides gone wild and in-laws who hate each other are part of everyday life. But this was celebrity clientele here. She couldn't part the crowd, step inside, and grab one of his ankles. One nudge from his size twenty-two sneaker could blast her to a chandelier. This could end up in the tabloids if handled wrong. Her heart skipped a beat when the cake wobbled. She thought fast, then whipped around to face the mother of the bride.

"Give me one minute."

Sara felt nervous as she headed for the band, and not just because of Cute New Guitar Guy. She had no idea if her little impromptu plan to save the cake was going to work. She'd worked with this cover band at many weddings and knew the lead singer, Kenny, well enough. He was cool for someone in his twenties, and he was really easy to work with. She stopped at the side of the stage and waved her arms. Kenny was too wrapped up in belting out Justin Timberlake to notice her. Then the guitarist's blue eyes landed on hers, and even in the midst of crisis she couldn't help but feel a buzz of warm, tingly excitement. Good thing it was a drum solo, because this gave Cute New Guitar Guy the opportunity to help her.

"I need Kenny!" She had to shout because the music was so loud she thought he wouldn't hear her. He gave her a very nonchalant thumbs-up, as if he was used to helping out in the middle of songs. He edged in close to

Kenny, made eye contact with the lead singer, then subtly nodded toward Sara.

Once she had Kenny's undivided attention, she mouthed, "CONGA LINE NOW. BEST MAN MUST LEAD."

Kenny closed in on his microphone. "Who's in the mood for a conga line?" His voice boomed over the crowd. There were a few howls from the dance floor. "Grab the waist of the closest person, and let's shake it up! I wanna see everyone on the dance floor! And I mean everyone! Where are the new Mr. and Mrs. Wilcox?" he sang. "I want the newlyweds in this conga line!"

She watched the bride scream, pull up her skirts, and jump to the front of the line. Her dress moved right along with the bridesmaids' as they began to dance around the room. "And where's the best man? Best man, I want you out there too," Kenny's voice sang through the microphone. "Everyone follow the best man."

Sara didn't have a chance to run for her life before Mickey Piper plucked her from the floor like a daisy and grabbed hold of her waist as he made her the head of the line. Her first thought was that she must look like a petrified leprechaun next to him.

The man was seven-two, which was a solid two feet taller than her minuscule frame.

"The conga line is the bomb!" Mickey shouted so loud she thought her ears would burst. When she'd suggested the conga line to Kenny, she never imagined that she'd end up in it. She tried to wiggle free, but his hands felt nailed to her waist. All she could do was move. Her biggest fear was that if she stopped, everyone would fall like dominoes behind her and she'd end up like gum beneath his shoe.

She didn't dance. She knew it was just the conga line, but she'd been watching things like this from the sidelines for years—not participating. Was she supposed to hop? Or did she trot? She took a few hops and felt her headset slip from the right side of her head. It dangled at an awkward angle over her forehead, and for a moment she was blind. She still held her clipboard. With one hand she grappled with the headset, but the moving train behind her pushed hard, and she only managed to get it away from her face. Somewhere in trying to fix the headset, her bangs had gotten caught in the wire, and her hair stuck up like weeds. She was the Easter Bunny with a lopsided ear.

She caught a glimpse of the caterer's son, Blake. He was usually the only other person her age working at events, and he thrived on flirtatiously teasing her. One glimpse of his delighted smile, and she knew that he had enough material to make fun of her for the rest of the summer. She thought she might die.

Clearly, hopping was not how it was done. She tried kicking each foot from side to side. All she could do was pray the song ended soon. She wished she'd run for her life before this hoops-throwing giant with a death grip got ahold of her. As they rounded the corner of the dance floor, her eyes landed on something truly nightmarish. Cute New Guitar Guy's gaze was aimed directly at her. A sly smile covered his face, and he nodded when their eyes caught. Hopping around the room like a moronic square dancer with a floppy headset and bangs standing on end would go down as one of the most embarrassing moments of her life.

Well, at least the cake had been saved. She hoped that the next time Mickey Piper chose to do the helicopter, he did it on the dance floor, away from all the expensive stuff. She felt her bangs flopping around and wondered if the situation could get any worse.

The first thing she did when the song ended was straighten her headset and fix her hair. Then she got as far away from Mickey Piper as she possibly could. She couldn't make eye contact with anyone in the room for fear of dying of embarrassment. It was hard to believe that it had only been minutes ago that she'd been praying for Cute New Guitar Guy to be around all summer. Now she sort of hoped she never saw him again. It was a good time to check in with her mother. Escape was welcome.

It would take a lot for her mother to ignore an RM alert. Sara imagined all kinds of catastrophes. Maybe that the filet mignon the bride had carefully selected had been confused by the caterer, and lobster covered each plate. Sara could still remember the bride explaining that her parents were deathly allergic to shellfish. The scent alone could trigger something called anaphylactic shock. Maybe her mom was desperately trying to come up with steaks in the last minutes before dinner, and that's why she hadn't answered.

There had to be a major explanation.

Get smitten with these scrumptious British treats:

Prada Princesses
by Jasmine Oliver

Three friends tackle
the high-stakes world
of fashion school.

10 Ways to Cope with Boys
by Caroline Plaisted

What every girl *really*
needs to know.

Does Snogging Count as Exercise?
by Helen Salter

For any girl who's
tongue-tied around boys.

From Simon Pulse · Published by Simon & Schuster

From **WILD** *to* **ROMANTIC**, don't miss these **PROM** stories from Simon Pulse!

A Really Nice Prom Mess

How I Created My
Perfect Prom Date

Prom Crashers

Prama

From Simon Pulse

• • •

Published by Simon & Schuster

From bestselling author
KATE BRIAN

♥ ♥ ♥ ♥ ♥

Juicy reads for the sweet and the sassy!

Sweet 16
As seen in *CosmoGIRL*!

Lucky T
"Fans of Meg Cabot's *The Princess Diaries* will enjoy it." —*SLJ*

Megan Meade's Guide to the McGowan Boys
Featured in *Teen* magazine!

The Virginity Club
"*Sex and the City: High School Edition.*" —*KLIATT*

The Princess & the Pauper
"Truly exceptional chick-lit." —*Kirkus Reviews*

FROM SIMON PULSE
♥ Published by Simon & Schuster ♥

"ONCE UPON A TIME"

is timely once again as fresh, quirky heroines breathe life into classic and much-loved characters.

Renowned heroines master newfound destinies, uncovering a unique and original **"happily ever after. . . ."**

BEAUTY SLEEP
Cameron Dokey

MIDNIGHT PEARLS
Debbie Viguié

SNOW
Tracy Lynn

WATER SONG
Suzanne Weyn

THE STORYTELLER'S DAUGHTER
Cameron Dokey

BEFORE MIDNIGHT
Cameron Dokey

GOLDEN
Cameron Dokey

THE ROSE BRIDE
Nancy Holder

From Simon Pulse
Published by Simon & Schuster